## "I'll see you at eight," Monroe said, breaking the standoff.

The sensation of his warm breath on her face gave Kim a ridiculously flushed and tingly feeling. The look in his eyes doubled that. What kind of boss was he? The kind who wouldn't mind breaking a few laws in order to get his way? The kind with a casting couch?

She broke eye contact. Her lashes fluttered. She stood there, helpless to get out of this, speechless for once, before backing up and turning abruptly.

She left Chaz Monroe, knowing that he stared after her, feeling his heated gaze. That scrutiny was so hot, she had an absurd longing to run back to him and press her mouth to his in a brief goodbye kiss, then laugh manically as she headed back to her cubicle to clear out her things.

The strangest bit of intuition told her he wanted that, too. In those insane moments of confrontation and unacceptable closeness, her senses screamed that Chaz Monroe had wanted to kiss her.

\* \* \*

If you're on Twitter,
tell us what you think of Harlequin Desire!
#harlequindesire

Dear Reader,

I'm really excited to be writing this note to you, and wow, in my favorite season of the year. So I wanted to tell you that it's thrills and chills for me to have my first Harlequin Desire book be a lighthearted holiday-themed romance, where two unsuspecting people meet up, clash and then ride that lightning bolt of over-the-top attraction toward their destiny.

I mean...could anything be better than finding love in all the wrong places?

In *The Boss's Mistletoe Maneuvers,* you'll be right there with Kim McKinley, a young advertising exec with a fear of embracing one particular holiday, and Chaz Monroe, her boss, who has to get to the heart of that problem in order to promote Kim to a position in his company that Kim not only dearly wants, but deserves. In the process of sorting things out, family secrets are revealed, and plenty of colorful sparks fly.

Just between us, I'll confess that Chaz Monroe is going to be a favorite of mine for a very long time. He has qualities that would melt my heart in a second, and the looks to match. I sure hope you'll fall for him the way I did. And since we can't actually have Chaz ourselves (sorry, girls!), root for Chaz and Kim to get together.

Because it's such a beautiful season for those of us who believe...in love.

Best wishes,

Linda

# THE BOSS'S MISTLETOE
# MANEUVERS

—

## LINDA THOMAS-SUNDSTROM

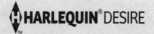

Recycling programs
for this product may
not exist in your area.

ISBN-13: 978-0-373-73352-1

The Boss's Mistletoe Maneuvers

**Printed in U.S.A.**

www.Harlequin.com

**Books by Linda Thomas-Sundstrom**

**Harlequin Desire**

*The Boss's Mistletoe Maneuvers* #2339

**Harlequin Nocturne**

*Red Wolf #81
*Wolf Trap #83
‡Golden Vampire #110
‡Guardian of the Night #137
  Immortal Obsession #192

*Wolf Moons
‡Vampire Moons

Other titles by this author available in ebook format.

---

# LINDA THOMAS-SUNDSTROM

Linda Thomas-Sundstrom writes contemporary romance and paranormal romance novels for the Harlequin Nocturne and Harlequin Desire lines. A teacher by day and a writer by night, Linda lives in the West, juggling teaching, writing, family and caring for a big stretch of land. She swears she has a resident Muse who sings so loudly, she often wears earplugs in order to get anything else done, but has big plans to eventually get to all those ideas.

Visit Linda's website: www.LindaThomas-Sundstrom.com

Connect on Facebook:

www.Facebook.com/LindaThomasSundstrom

# One

Chaz Monroe knew a great female backside when he saw one. And the blonde with the swinging ponytail walking down the hallway in front of him was damn near a ten.

Lean, rounded, firm and feminine, her admirable backside swayed from side to side as she moved, above the short hemline of a tight black skirt that did little to hide a great pair of legs. Long, shapely legs, encased in paperthin black tights and ending in a pair of perfectly sensible black leather pumps.

The sensible pumps were a disappointment and a slight hiccup in his rating overall, given the sexiness of the rest of her. She was red stilettos all the way, Chaz decided. Satin shoes maybe, or suede. Still, though the woman was a visual sensory delight, now wasn't the time or place for an indulgence of that kind. Not with an employee. Never with an employee.

She wore a blue fuzzy sweater that molded to her slender torso and was on the tall side of small. Her stride was purposeful, businesslike and almost arrogant in the way she maneuvered through the narrow hallway, skillfully avoiding chairs, unused consoles and the watercooler. Her heels made soft clicking sounds that didn't echo much.

Chaz followed her until she turned right, heading for Cubicle City. At that junction, as he hooked a left toward his new office, he caught a whiff of scent that lingered in her wake. Not a typical floral fragrance, either. Something subtle, almost sweet, that would have decided her fate right then and there if he'd been another kind of guy, with a different sort of agenda.

This guy had to think and behave like the new owner of an advertising agency in the heart of Manhattan.

Taking over a new business required the kind of time that ruled out relationships, including dates and dalliances. In the past two months he'd become a freaking monk, since there wasn't one extra hour in his schedule for distractions if he was to turn this company around in a decent amount of time. That was the priority. All of his money was riding on this company making it. He'd spent every cent he had to buy this advertising firm.

Whistling, Chaz strolled past Alice Brody, his newly inherited pert, big-eyed, middle-aged, fluffy-haired executive secretary. He entered his office through a set of glass doors still bearing the name of the vice president he'd already had to let go for allowing the company to slowly slide from the top of the heap to the mediocre middle. Lackluster management was unacceptable in a company where nothing seemed to be wrong with the work of the rest of the staff.

"There is one more person to see today," Alice called after him.

"Need a few minutes to go over some things first," Chaz said over his shoulder. "Can you bring in the file I asked for?"

"I'll get on it right away."

Something in Alice's tone made him wonder what she might be thinking. He could feel her eyes on him. When he glanced back at her, she smiled.

Chaz shrugged off the thought, used to women liking his looks. But his older brother Rory was the real catch. As the first self-made millionaire in the family, his brother made headlines and left trails of women in his wake.

Chaz had a lot of catching up to do to match his brother's magic with a floundering company. So there were, at the moment, bigger fish to fry.

First up, he had to finish dealing with old contract issues

and get everyone up to speed with the new company plan. He had to decide how to speak to one person in particular. Kim McKinley, the woman highly recommended by everyone here for an immediate promotion. The woman in line for the VP job before he had temporarily taken over that office, going undercover in this new business as an employee.

More to the point, he had to find out why Kim McKinley had a clause in her contract that excluded her from working on the biggest advertising campaign of the year. *Christmas*.

He couldn't see how an employee headed for upper management could be exempt from dealing with Christmas campaigns, when it was obvious she was a player, otherwise.

He'd done his homework and had made it a priority to find out about Kim, who spearheaded four of the company's largest accounts. Her clients seemed to love her. They threw money at her, and this was a good thing.

He could use someone like this by his side, and was confident that he could make her see reason about the Christmas campaigns. Intelligent people had to be flexible. It would be a shame to issue an ultimatum, if it came to that, for Kim to lose what she had worked so hard for because of his new rules on management and contracts.

Chaz picked up a pencil and tucked it behind his ear, knowing by the way it stuck there easily that he needed a haircut, and that haircuts were a luxury when business came first.

He was sure that his upcoming appointment with Kim McKinley would turn out well. Handling people was what he usually did best when he took over a new company in his family's name. Juggling this agency's problems and getting more revenue moving in the right direction was the reason he had bought this particular firm for himself. That, and the greedy little need to show his big brother what he could do on his own.

The agency's bottom line wasn't bad; it just needed some TLC. Which was why he had gone undercover as the new VP. He figured it would be easier for other employees to deal with a fellow employee, rather than an owner. Even an employee in management. Pretending to be one of them for a while would give him a leg up on the internal workings of the business.

He would be good to Kim McKinley and all of the others who wanted to work and liked it here, if they played ball.

Did they have to love him? *No.*

But he'd hopefully earn their respect.

Chaz turned when the door opened, and Alice breezed in without knocking. She handed over a manila file folder held together with a thick rubber band. Thanking her, he waited until she left before sitting down. Centering the file on his desk, he read the name on it.

*Kimberly McKinley.*

He removed the rubber band, opened the folder and read the top page. She was twenty-four years old, had graduated from NYU with honors.

He already knew most of that.

He skimmed through the accolades. She was described as a hard worker. An honest, inventive, intelligent, creative self-starter with a good client base. An excellent earner recommended for advancement to a position in upper management.

A handwritten scribble in the margins added, *Lots of bang for the buck.*

There was one more thing he wished he could check in the file, for no other reason than a passing interest. Her marital status. Single people were known for their work ethics and the extra hours they could put in. McKinley's quick rise in the company was probably due not only to her ability to reel in business and keep it, but also to her availability.

What could be better than that?

He stole a glance at the empty seat across from him then looked again at the overstuffed folder. He tapped his fingers on the desk. "How badly do you want a promotion, Kim?" he might ask her. The truth was that if she were to get that promotion, she'd be one of the youngest female vice presidents in the history of advertising.

And that was fine with him. Young minds were good minds, and McKinley truly sounded like the embodiment of the name her coworkers had given her. *Wonder Woman.*

Although he was already familiar with her tally of clients, he checked over the list.

Those four clients that he'd classify as the Big Four, refused to work with anyone else, and it was a sure bet McKinley knew this, too, and would possibly use it as leverage if push came to shove about her taking on holiday-themed campaigns that didn't suit her. Would those clients turn away if he accidentally pushed McKinley too hard, and she walked? Rumor had it that three of them had been hoping she'd add Christmas to her list and stop farming those holiday accounts out.

He looked up to find Alice again in the doorway, as if the woman had psychically picked up on his need to ask questions.

"What will Kim have to say about believing she has been passed over in favor of me in this office?" was his first one.

Alice, through highly glossed ruby lips, said, "Kim had been promised the job by the last guy behind that desk. She'll be disappointed."

"How disappointed?"

"Very. She's an asset to this company. It would be a shame to lose her."

Chaz nodded thoughtfully. "You think she might leave?"

Alice shrugged. "It's a possibility. I can name a few other agencies in the city that would like to have her onboard."

Chaz glanced at the file, supposing he was going to have

to wear kid gloves when he met McKinley. If everyone else in town wanted her, how would pressure tactics work in getting her to stay put and take on more work?

He nodded to Alice, the only staff member who knew what his real agenda was for playing at being the new VP, and that he now owned everything from the twelfth to the fourteenth floor.

"Why doesn't she do Christmas campaigns?" he asked.

"I have no idea. It must be something personal," Alice replied. "She'll attend meetings when necessary, but doesn't handle the actual work."

"Why do you think it might be personal?" Chaz pressed.

"Take a look at her cubicle."

"Is something wrong with it?"

"There's nothing Christmasy about it. It's fifteen days until the big holiday, and she doesn't possess so much as a red and green pen," Alice said.

An image of the blonde in the hallway crowded his mind as if tattooed there. He wondered if Kim McKinley would be anything like that. He tended to picture McKinley as a stern, no-nonsense kind of a gal. Glasses, maybe, and a tweed suit to make her seem older than her actual age and give her some street cred.

"Thanks, Alice."

"My pleasure," Alice said, closing the door as she exited.

Chaz leaned back in his chair and scanned the office, thinking he'd like to be anywhere but there, undercover. Pretending wasn't his forte. To his credit, he had been a pretty decent young advertising exec himself a few years back, before entering the family business of buying up companies. In the time since then, he'd made more than one flustered employee cry.

He was responsible for the decisions regarding the upper echelon of this agency. But once he revealed he was the new owner, the future occupant of the VP's office would require more than a rave review on paper and a few happy clients. He found it inconceivable that anyone considered for such a promotion would avoid working on campaigns that brought in big revenue for the company. What was Kim McKinley thinking?

Chaz swiveled toward the window, where he had a bird's-eye view of the street below. Though it was already dark outside, he got to his feet and peered out, counting four Santas on street corners collecting for charity in a city that was draped in holiday trappings.

When the knock came on his door, Chaz looked around. He wasn't expecting anyone for another hour, and Alice never bothered to announce her own entrance. The thought that someone could bypass Alice seemed ludicrous.

The knock came again. After one more sharp rap, the doorknob moved. It seemed that his visitor wasn't going to wait for permission to come in.

The door swung open. A woman, her outline exaggerated by the lights behind her, straddled the threshold in a slightly imperious stance.

"You wanted to see me?" the woman said.

Chaz figured this could only be the notorious McKinley, since she was the only person left on his list to see that day.

After realizing she wasn't actually going to take a single step into the room, he blew out a long, low breath without realizing he'd been holding it, and squelched the urge to laugh out loud.

Had he wished too hard for this, maybe, and someone had been listening?

The woman in his doorway was none other than the delicious blonde.

Yep, *that* one.

*"The* Kim McKinley?" the man by the window said.

Kim was so angry, she could barely control herself. Her hand on the doorknob shook with irritation.

"You wanted to see me?" she repeated.

"Yes. Please come in," he said from behind the desk that should have been hers. "Have a seat."

She shook her head. "I doubt if I'll be here long enough to get comfortable."

This was an unfortunate double entendre. Chaz Monroe was either going to praise her or hand her a pink slip for being his closest competition.

With a familiar dread knotting her stomach, she added, "I have a pressing appointment that might last for some time."

"I won't keep you long. Please, Miss McKinley, come in."

She stood her ground. "I have a tight schedule to maintain today, Mr. Monroe, and I came here to ask if we can have our sit-down appointment at a later time?"

She had been expecting this talk from the new guy, but truly hadn't expected *this*. His looks. The shock of seeing the usurper in the flesh held her in place, and kept her at a slight disadvantage. At the moment, she couldn't have moved from the doorway if she'd tried.

For once, rumors hadn't lied. Chaz Monroe was a hunk. Not only was he younger than she had imagined, he was also incredibly handsome…though he was, she reminded herself, in *her* office.

This newcomer had been handed the job she had been promised, and he'd summoned her as if she were a minion. He stood behind the mahogany desk like a king, impeccably dressed, perfectly gorgeous and not at all as rigid as she had anticipated he would be.

In fact, he looked downright at home. Already.

She stared openly at him.

Shaggy dark hair, deep brown, almost black, surrounded an angular face. Light eyes—blue maybe, she couldn't be sure—complemented his long-sleeved, light blue shirt. He flashed a sensual smile full of enviable white teeth, but the smile had to be phony. They both knew he was going to gloss over the fact that he'd gotten this job, in her place, if he'd done any research at all. He no doubt would also ask about the Christmas clause in her contract, first thing, without knowing anything about her. He'd try to put her in her place, and on the defensive. She felt this in her bones.

A shiver of annoyance passed through her.

She was willing to bet that this guy was good at lording over people. He had that kind of air. Monroe was a devil in a dashing disguise, and if she didn't behave, if she said what was really on her mind, she'd be jobless in less than ten minutes.

"Did you want something in particular?" she asked.

"I wanted to get acquainted. I've heard a lot about you, and I have a few questions about your file," Monroe said, his eyes moving over her intently as he spoke. He was studying her, too. Maybe he searched for a chink in her armor.

She'd be damned if she'd let him find it.

A trickle of perspiration dripped between Kim's shoulder blades, caused by the dichotomy of weighing Monroe's looks against what he was going to do to her when she refused to play nice with him. Maybe it wasn't his fault that she'd been passed over for the promotion, but did he have to look so damn content?

And if he were to push her about her contract?

Monroe had only been in this building for two days, while her guilt about Christmas was years-old and remained depressingly fresh. Her mother had died only six months ago; it hadn't been long enough for Kim to get over the years of darkness about the Christmas holidays that had prevailed in the McKinley household.

Kim shut her eyes briefly to regroup and felt awkward seconds ticking by.

"Please come in. If you're in a hurry, let's talk briefly about the Christmas stuff," he said, verifying her worst fears.

"If it's the Christmas files you want, you'll need to see Brenda Chang," she said coolly. "Brenda's the one down the hall with the decorated cubicle. Red paper, garlands, tinsel, and holiday carols on CD. You can't miss it. Brenda oversees some of the December holiday ads."

She watched Monroe circle to the front of the desk, where he sat on the edge and indicated the vacant chair beside him with a wave of his hand. *Just a friendly little chat...*

Refusing to oblige his regal fantasies, Kim stubbornly remained in the doorway, anxiously screwing the heel of one shoe into the costly beige Berber carpet.

He maintained eye contact in a way that made her slightly dizzy from the intensity of his stare. "And you don't have any Christmas accounts, why, exactly? If you're one of the best we've got, shouldn't you be overseeing our biggest source of revenue?"

"Thanks for the compliment, but I don't do this particular holiday. I'm sure it's all there in my file. I can help Alice locate my contract before I go, if you'd like."

Monroe's calm, professional expression didn't falter. "Perhaps you can explain why you don't *do* Christmas? I'd honestly like to know."

"It's personal. Plus, I'm very busy doing other work here." Kim held up a hand. "Look, I'd love to have this get-acquainted chat." The words squeezed through tight lips. "But I'll have to beg off right now. I'm sorry. I really am expected somewhere."

"It's almost five. Do you have a work-related appointment?" Monroe asked.

Kim started to ask what business it was of his, then thought better of voicing such a thing because like it or not, he was her boss, and it was his business. She had agreed to meet some friends for a quick drink in the bar downstairs, and it was important that she got home right after that, before the beautiful holiday lights made her think again and more seriously about dishonoring her mother's memory.

Lately, she'd been having second thoughts about what she'd experienced growing up, and what she'd been taught, both about the insensitivity of men and the pain of the holidays.

Her mother hadn't approved of anything to do with Christmas. For the McKinleys, Christmas meant sorrow and the extremes of loss. It meant sad memories of a husband and father who had deserted his wife and five-year-old daughter on Christmas Eve to be with another family.

Kim looked at Monroe levelly. No way she was going to tell him any of that, and she shouldn't have to dredge up the details of something that had already been hammered out a year ago when she negotiated her contract with somebody else on this floor.

"Sure, meeting later would be fine," Monroe said. "Maybe around eight?"

"I'm usually in by seven, so yes, I can return first thing in the morning if that's what you'd like," Kim said.

"Actually, I meant tonight. 8:00 p.m.," he clarified, enunciating clearly. "If it wouldn't be too terribly inconvenient, that is, and you're still around. We can keep it casual and meet in the bar downstairs. That's not too much out of the way, right?"

"The bar?" Kim heard the slip in her tone.

"In the bar, yes," he said, without losing the charming, almost boyish smile.

*Damn him.* It was a really nice smile.

"I'm told it's a regular meeting place after hours for employees," he continued. "Maybe we can snag a quiet table?"

So they could do what? Have a friendly drink before the ax fell? Before the arguments began?

*Don't think so.*

"Will you be finished with your appointment by then?" Monroe pressed.

Realizing that she couldn't lie, and since others from the agency were going to be in that same bar, and still might be hanging around at eight, she said, "Yes," adding in another job-related double entendre, "I'll be finished."

With those last three words dangling between them, Chaz Monroe got to his feet and walked right up to her.

She had to wince to keep from backing up.

He came very close. Obviously, he had no intention of preserving her tiny circle of personal space.

Then he invaded it.

And hell…

Up close, he was even better.

"Your appointment isn't a date?" he asked in a husky tone that wasn't at all businesslike.

Kim felt breathless so close to this incredibly gorgeous guy who was her new boss, and chastised herself for being affected by him in such a physical way. Monroe was a time bomb comprised of every woman's sexual addictions, from his shaggy hair to his loafered feet. In order to become desensitized to this kind of personal frontal attack, she'd have had to experience quite a few near misses in the past with men of Monroe's caliber.

No such thing was in her dating history.

Her feet inched forward to close the distance to him before she could stop them. Her breasts strained at her sweater with a reaction so unacceptable, she wanted to scream. But she heard herself say, "Not tonight. No date."

The words *wrong* and *harassment* sailed through her mind. He was close enough to touch. Why?

He was also near enough to punch, but she didn't take a swing.

Chaz Monroe was a head taller than she was and smelled like *man,* in a really good way. He radiated sex appeal and an easy, unattended elegance. He didn't wear a coat or a tie, yet what he did wear was confidence, in an unintimidating manner. His casualness was reflected in the fact that his shirt was open at the neck, revealing a triangle of bare, lightly tanned skin. That taut, masculine flesh captured her attention for what seemed like several long minutes before she glanced up....

To meet his blue eyes.

That's when she heard music.

She shook her head, not quite believing it, but the music didn't go away. It was Christmas music, she finally realized, coming from the lobby and signaling the nearness of closing time for most of the staff. She had to get out of there and was caught between a rock and...a hard body.

"Good. I'll see you at eight," Monroe said, breaking the standoff.

The sensation of his warm breath on her face gave Kim a ridiculously flushed and tingly few seconds. The look in his eyes doubled that. What kind of boss was he? The kind that wouldn't mind breaking a few laws in order to get his way? The kind with a casting couch?

Had her mother been right about overly attractive men being saps, after all?

She broke eye contact. Her lashes fluttered.

"Eight o'clock. In the bar," he said in a tone that gave her an electrical jolt and made her clothing feel completely inadequate as a barrier against the sleek, seductive hoodoo he had going on.

Excuses for her reaction beat at her from the inside. The air around her visibly trembled with the need to shout "Go to hell!" Yet she stood there, helpless to get out of this, speechless for once, before backing up and turning abruptly.

She left Chaz Monroe, knowing that he stared after her, feeling his heated gaze. That scrutiny was so hot, she had an absurd longing to run back to him and get it over with. Just press her mouth to his in a brief goodbye kiss, then laugh maniacally as she headed back to her cubicle to clear out her things.

The strangest bit of intuition told her that he wanted that same thing. In those insane moments of confrontation and unacceptable closeness, her senses screamed that Chaz Monroe had wanted to kiss her.

She knew something else, as well. Because of the fire in her nerve endings and the way her heart thundered, meeting Chaz Monroe at the bar tonight was a very…bad…idea.

# Two

Chaz faced the distinct possibility of being in serious trouble before Kim McKinley had left him standing in the open doorway. He had very nearly just breached every rule of decorum in the book. Well, he had thought about it, anyway.

She hadn't helped any.

Resisting the urge to loosen his collar, which was already loosened, he cleared his throat and looked to Alice, who was watching him with a raised eyebrow. Only practice allowed him to keep his expression neutral when he felt an annoying shudder in the abs he had worked so hard on in the gym before his takeover of this company shot down his regular routine.

Nodding to Alice, he stepped back into his office.

"Damn."

He had gotten up close and personal with an employee. His idea to dish some of that haughty attitude of McKinley's right back at her had backfired, big-time.

Not only were her body and her sexy scent tantalizing as hell, Kim's face and voice were undeniably appetizing. She had an accent, a slight Southern drawl that resulted in a slow drawing out of syllables. Her voice was deep, sultry and a lot like whispered vibrations passing through overheated air.

As for her face...

It was the face of an angel. The pale, silky-smooth, slightly babyish oval wasn't in any way indicative of her crisp attitude.

He could feel the residual intensity of her expressive hazel eyes, and didn't even want to think about her lips.

Pink lips, moist, slick and slightly parted, as if just waiting to be kissed.

Chaz touched his forehead absently. Hell, if he didn't have a bone to pick with her over the Christmas stuff, and if he actually relied on first impressions of a physical nature, he'd have been tempted to throw in the towel and give her the office right then and there—anything to get closer to her.

*Anything to taste those lips.*

*Man.* His mind had taken an inconvenient slip, a sudden, unexpected detour, and he wanted to laugh at the situation and at himself. However, there was more to be considered here. If he was going to be around Kim McKinley on a regular basis, he'd have to be able to keep his mind on business; a real feat, given the outline of the world-class breasts he'd seen through the thin layer of cloud-blue cashmere.

Damn it, why hadn't anyone told him about *that?*

Returning to the desk, pulling the pencil from behind his ear, Chaz scratched *Personnel files should contain all pertinent information in the future* on a yellow notepad.

Tapping the pencil on McKinley's file, he vowed not to debate with himself about what a pouty mouth like hers might do, other than kissing, while realizing that X-rated thoughts had no place in contract negotiations or the boardroom.

He shook his head. In spite of the untimely, if temporary, dilemma, Chaz didn't lose the smile when he looked again to the doorway where Kim had just stood, cute as a bug from the neck up and devilishly delicious from the neck down, while she made a decent attempt at blowing him off.

*Can we talk later?*

*I have a schedule to keep to.*

Kim McKinley, it seemed, wasn't going to take losing this office well. She was angry and trying to deal. It was possible that as long as she remained on his payroll, thinking he had the job she coveted, she might do everything in her power to either avoid him or bust his chops.

True, he had pushed her a little, and hadn't explained what he was doing here, undercover—which would have defeated the purpose of being undercover.

Could she really be so good at her job? She might be decent at what she did for this agency and damn nice to look at, but no one was so indispensable that they could afford to anger the new man in charge within the first sixty seconds of meeting him.

Yet that's just what she had done. Sort of.

Reopening her file, Chaz pondered the question of whether she had actually just offered up a challenge. Had McKinley meant to wave a flag in front of the bull, a flag bearing the legend *Leave me alone, or lose me?*

The back of Chaz's neck prickled the way it usually did when the anticipation of a good challenge set in. This particular tickle was similar to the feelings he'd had when he had handed over ten million dollars for a company he had every intention of making more successful than it was before he stepped in. The tickle was also similar to the one brought about by thoughts of the self-imposed challenge of tackling his brother's track record of successful takeovers, and proving his own business acumen.

Testy employees had no place in either of those particular goals, except for doing the jobs assigned to them. He really could not afford to be distracted right now.

Chaz stared at the door, where Kim McKinley had drawn an invisible battle line on several levels. His mind buzzed with possibilities. Maybe she used her looks to get what she wanted, and that was part of her success. It could be that she believed herself to be so valuable that he wouldn't mess with her if she resisted his logical suggestions.

Or if she resisted his advances.

*What? Damn.* He hadn't just thought that. *Advances* were totally out of the question.

Sitting down in his chair, Chaz placed both hands on the desk, disgusted that he'd been waylaid by this surprise. Kim McKinley just wasn't what he had expected, that's all. And the firm could always find someone to replace her if her attitude got out of hand.

Was that a fair assessment of the situation?

As he tapped his pencil on her file, he mulled over the fact that she had avoided their first sit-down appointment. Did she consider that a point for her side? Would she believe she had racked up another point for failing to give him any of the information he had been seeking, or meeting his demands on that Christmas clause head-on?

Was she the type to keep score?

Chaz rubbed the back of his neck where the darn prickle of interest just wouldn't ease up. Buttoning the collar of his shirt, he firmed up his resolve to get to the bottom of the McKinley mystery. Wonder Woman would be wrong if she thought him a fool. He was a master at compartmentalizing when he had to. He hadn't gotten to where he was in business by tossing employees on the carpet according to whim, or dumping their sorry backsides in the street without real cause. He was bigger than that, and he always played fair.

He would meet Kim McKinley tonight and set things straight. He'd give her the benefit of the doubt about adhering to his company plan, and get her onboard, whatever it took to do so.

"Your contract. No question marks. Not up for negotiation."

He practiced those words aloud, repeated them less forcefully and set his mental agenda.

The bar, in three hours.

They'd have a friendly chat and get to the specifics of the deal. McKinley might turn out to be a good ally.

*As for the bedroom dreams...*

He let out a bark of self-deprecating laughter over the time he was spending on this one issue, a sure sign that truly, and admittedly, he hadn't been prepared for the likes of this woman.

He really would have to be more cautious in the future, because, man-oh-man, what he needed right that minute, in Kim McKinley's saucy Southern wake, and in preparation for meeting her again was...

...a very long, very cold shower.

Kim tumbled into her chair and laid her head down on her desk. She turned just far enough to eye the golden plaque perched next to her pencil sharpener that had been a gift from her friend Brenda.

*Kim McKinley, VP of Advertising.*

"Some joke." She backhanded the plaque, sending it sailing. Who had she been kidding, anyway? Vice president? A twenty-four-year-old *woman?*

There would be no big office with floor-to-ceiling windows in her immediate future. No maple shelving for potted plants, and no opportunity to implement her plans and ideas for the company. So didn't she feel exactly like that jettisoned plaque—shot into space, only to land with a dismal thud right back in her own six-by-six cubicle?

Could the moisture welling up in her eyes be *tears?* As in about to *cry* tears?

*Unacceptable.*

Twenty-four-year-old professionals didn't blubber away when they were royally disappointed, or when they were overlooked and underappreciated at the office.

*No tears. No way. No how.*

She was mad, that's all, with no way to express how sad she was going to be if she had to leave this building and everything she had built here in the past five years.

"Why does everyone want to push me about the damn contract?" she grumbled, figuring that Brenda, in the next cubicle, would be listening. "Haven't I worked extremely hard on every other blasted campaign all year long? I've all but slept in this cubicle. I keep clothes in my desk drawers. Would it be fair to dock me over one single previously negotiated item?"

Inhaling damp desk blotter and the odor of evergreen that now pervaded the building, Kim reviewed the proverbial question on the table.

*Was there another person on earth who could say that Christmas had been their downfall?*

Plunking her head again on the desk, she muttered a weak "ouch." Rustling up some anger didn't seem to be working at the moment. It was obvious that she needed more work on self-defense.

"You okay?" a voice queried from somewhere behind her. "I heard a squeak."

Kim blinked.

"Kim? Are you, or are you not okay?"

"Nope. Not okay." She didn't bother to sit up.

"Are you in need of medical attention?"

Moving her mouth with difficulty because it was stuck to some paper, Kim said, "Intravenous Success Serum would be helpful. Got any?"

"No, but I've got something even better."

"Valium? Hemlock? A place with cheap rent?"

"An invitation to have drinks with the new boss tonight in the bar just arrived by email."

Kim muffled a scream. What had Brenda just said? They were both to have drinks with *Monroe?* The bastard had invited a crowd to witness her third degree and possible dismissal?

"Now's not a good time, Bren," she said. Having a coworker for her best friend sometimes had its drawbacks.

Like their close proximity when she wanted to pout by herself.

"I think now would be a good time, actually," Brenda countered. "We can find out what the new guy is like, en masse."

"I'll tell you what he's like in one word. *Brutus!*"

Brenda stuck her head over the partition separating their cubicles. "I'm guessing your meeting didn't go well?"

Kim pried her cheek from the desk, narrowed her eyes and turned to face Brenda.

"So not afraid of that look," Brenda said.

"That's the problem. Neither was he."

"Yes, well, didn't you just know that the damn Christmas clause was going to jump up and bite you again someday? I mean how could they understand when they don't know...."

Kim held up a hand that suggested if Brenda said one more word along those lines, she might regret it.

"I've probably just lost my dream job, Bren. For all intents and purposes, this agency considers me an ancestor of old mister Scrooge. And by the way, aren't best friends supposed to offer sympathy in times of crisis, without lengthy lectures tacked on?"

Not much taller than the five foot partition in her bare feet, Brenda, who went shoeless in her space, was barely visible. All that showed was a perfectly straight center part halving a swath of shiny black hair, and a pair of kohl-lined, almond-shaped eyes. The eyes were shining merrily. There might have been a piece of tinsel entwined in a few ebony strands near Brenda's forehead.

What Brenda lacked in stature, however, she made up for in persistence. "I might suggest that nobody will believe that anyone actually hates Christmas, Kim. Not for real."

Brenda didn't stop there. "That's what the new guy will be thinking. So maybe you can come up with an alternate reason for holding back on the holiday stuff that he will buy into. Like…religious reasons."

"Seriously?" Sarcasm returned to Kim's tone as she offered Brenda what she thought was a decent rendition of a go-away-and-leave-me-alone-or-else look.

Brenda performed a glossy hair flip. "Still not afraid," she said. "Or discouraged."

Kim got to her feet and smoothed her skirt over her hips. "I think it's already too late for help of any kind."

"Tell me about it," Brenda said. "But first you have to dish about whether Monroe really does have a nice ass."

Kim kneaded the space between her eyes with shaky fingers, trying to pinpoint the ache building there.

"You didn't think he was hot?" Brenda continued. "That's the word going around. H-o-t, as in *fan yourself*."

"Yeah? Did you hear anything about the man being an arrogant idiot?" Kim asked.

"No. My sources might have left that part out."

"I don't actually care about the nice ass part, Bren. I prefer not to notice an area that I won't be kissing."

"Don't be absurd, Kim. No one expects you to kiss anyone's backside. It isn't professional. What happened?"

"I'll have to start over somewhere else, that's what. Monroe won't let me off the hook. He expects me to explain everything. He'll expect me to cave." She waved both hands in the air. "I can't tell him about my background. I can barely talk about it to myself."

"You told me."

"That's different. Best friends are best friends. How I grew up isn't any of his business."

"What about the fact that you've been wanting to forget about this issue with your family for some time now, anyway?" Brenda asked. "Maybe it's the right time to take that next step."

Kim couldn't find the words to address Brenda's remark. She wondered if anyone really knew how bad guilt trips felt and how deep some family issues went, if they hadn't experienced it.

She had a hole inside her that hadn't completely closed over and was filled with heartaches that had had plenty of time to fester at a cellular level. Her mother had constantly reminded her of how they'd been wronged by a man, and about the dishonest things all men do for utterly selfish reasons.

Her mom wouldn't listen to advice about getting help in order to emergé from under the dark clouds surrounding her traumatic marital disappointment. Instead, she had spread those dark clouds over Kim.

The guilt about wanting to be rid of the deep-seated feelings of abandonment was sharp-edged, and nearly as painful now as the old heartaches. The warnings her mother had given her had calloused several times over.

Kim had thought long and hard about this since her mother's death. What she had needed was a little more leeway to get used to the fact that with her mother gone, she could embrace change without angering or hurting anyone else. Still, did that entail capitulating on the Christmas issue so soon? Was she ready for that, when this particular holiday had played such a negative role in her life?

Brenda hurried on. "If you don't want to tell Monroe the truth, you have about an hour to formulate a reason he'll accept in lieu of the truth. Fabricating illusions is what we do on a daily basis, right? We make people want to buy things."

After letting a beat of time go by for that to sink in, Brenda spoke again. "Call me selfish, Kim, but I'd like to keep you here and happy, and so would a whole host of other people. I doubt if the new guy would actually fire you, anyway. He'd have no real reason to. You can work this out. Also, you could try the truth. Talking about it might be cathartic."

Kim shook her head. Brenda hadn't witnessed Monroe's show of personalized aggression in his office doorway. Monroe had used the physical card to get her to back down, intending to intimidate her with his stockpile of charisma. And it had worked. There was no way she'd talk to a complete stranger about complicated and painful personal details and have him laugh them off as childish. Or worse, have him wave them away as being inconsequential.

"If the truth is still too painful, maybe you can spin the issue another way." Brenda snorted delicately. "You could tell Monroe that you have a Santa fetish."

Kim gave her a look.

"You can tell him a therapist explained that your Santa fetish means that you're looking for a father figure to replace yours, and you've attached yourself to a fantasy ideal. So much so, that it's embarrassing to discuss or work with."

Kim knew a ploy to lighten the mood when she heard one.

"Bren, you are usually so much better than that."

"The source of the idea wouldn't matter, Kim. Mention the word *therapist,* and Monroe would be afraid of a lawsuit if he were to ever fire you for mental health reasons."

Brenda had the audacity to giggle, despite the seriousness of the subject matter, because she was on a ludicrous roll. "You secretly long for the person who is supposed to possess magical powers that he uses for good, and this longing makes you crazy at this time of year."

"Bren, listen to yourself. You're suggesting that I tell my boss I have a secret hard-on for the guy whose belly shakes like a bowlful of jelly, and reindeer with dorky names."

"Humor aside, isn't that what you're actually waiting for? Haven't you been searching for a man with the ability to override your background issues by making dull things seem shiny and bright? You'd like to find an honest man

who could disprove your mother's ideas about relationships."

Kim rubbed her forehead harder. Brenda was right. She
did want a man with those quasi-magical qualities. Someone caring, understanding, strong and above all, loyal. She
got breathless just thinking about it, and about separating
herself from the dark spell her mother had woven.

The problem was, she seemed to only date men who had
none of those things to offer. Every one of her companions
so far had come up short of ideal. Maybe she'd made her
poor choices to subconsciously confirm her mother's phi-
losophy of relationship instability and injustice. She could
see this. It made sense. Honestly though, she did not want
to end up alone, and like her mother.

She sagged against the wall. "There's a fatal flaw in your
reasoning, Bren. If I had a desire for Santa Claus and his
magic, why would I be opposed to working on Christmas?
I'd love Christmas. But you are partly right."

Kim pressed the hair back from her face and continued. "Secretly, I've always wanted to dump the darkness
and embrace the holiday celebrations. I've wanted that for
as long as I can remember. It's been my secret heartache."

More to the point, she couldn't stand anger and blame
and insidious hatred, and had missed a good portion of her
childhood fantasies because of her mother's take on those
things. The idea of a real Santa Claus had been her one on-
going illicit passion from early on. A dream. A ray of light
in the dark world she'd grown up in.

She had never disclosed this secret longing to anyone.
What good would it do? What child didn't want to lighten
the load and share celebrations with her friends, in spite of
the fact that some things were forbidden?

Guilt was a desperate emotion. Its tentacles ran deep
and clung hard. Nevertheless, contrary to her mother's feelings, she had never wanted to commit her father to the

fires of Hades for making her mother's life miserable. For Kim, there had only been sadness, emptiness. Little girls needed their fathers.

She had grown up desiring the ability to absorb pain, table it and move on. She wished to fill the emptiness inside her with something better than loss. Creativity had done that for her. This job had done it. She made other peoples' fantasies come true on a regular basis. Just not hers.

Not that one specific fantasy, anyway.

"I want to participate in the holiday festivities and be really truly happy," she confessed. "I just don't know how to go about it, or where to start. I'm afraid my mother might roll over in her grave if I did."

As for the theory of cheating men, wrong men…that image seemed to fit the new boss, Chaz Monroe. Although she'd had tingly feelings in his presence, and her heart rate had skyrocketed, all that proved was that her pattern of choosing inappropriate males hadn't ended. She was attracted to flighty men caught up in their own needs. If she went down that particular path, led by Chaz Monroe, she'd regret it.

"I'm considering shock treatment," she said. "I don't rule it out."

"To my way of thinking, a little therapy now might save you a load of trouble in the long run," Brenda agreed. "Please don't be mad that I'm telling you this. Friends have obligations."

Way too much time had been spent on this. Kim could hear her watch ticking.

Brenda sighed. "There is always plan B. If you don't want to discuss this tonight, you could distract him. Throw Monroe a curveball. A sexy new outfit and some killer shoes worn as a talisman against unwanted negativity might work. At least it might give you another day or two to decide what to do."

"I didn't know shoes could repel negativity."

"They can if they're the red stilettos in the window of the shop next door."

"Those shoes cost more than my rent."

"Won't they be worth it if they work?" Brenda pointed out.

"If they don't, will you pay my bills?"

"I have a little cash saved up," Brenda admitted.

Kim tried not to choke on the Tree In A Can spray coming from Brenda's cubicle. She didn't want to bring Brenda down with her. The fact was that this new boss was likely going to create some havoc, and she'd have to wiggle her way out of the situation in order to prolong her employment. Chaz Monroe hadn't seemed like the kind of guy who was used to compromises.

Was Monroe a jerk? Maybe. He'd wanted to make her uncomfortable with all that forbidden closeness, and his method had scored. Worse yet, he had seen her squirm. If he got close to her again, though, she'd cry foul, in public, where she'd have witnesses to his behavior.

Oh yes, Chaz Monroe, playboy, would be trouble, all right.

"He has big blue eyes," she said wistfully, then looked to Brenda, hoping she hadn't just announced that out loud.

"Then there's nothing to worry about," Brenda concluded. "Because real demons have red eyes. And tails."

A chill trickled down Kim's spine, messing with the heat left over from her meeting with Monroe. Misplaced heat waves aside, the real question was whether she wanted to keep this job, and the answer was yes. No one wanted to find out how long the unemployment lines would be in December. Plus, she truly liked most of the people she worked with.

So…could she afford to allow Christmas to be a deal breaker, or was she willing to fight for what she wanted?

"A sexy dress and some shoes, huh?" she said.

Brenda nodded. "It's a bit aggressive, but it's been done for ages. Think Mata Hari."

Kim tilted her head in thought.

"Uh-oh," Brenda said, disappearing from behind the partition and appearing in the entrance to Kim's cubicle. "I don't think I like what I see in your eyes."

"I don't know what you mean."

"You wouldn't do anything stupid, right, like trying to seduce Monroe out of his title?" Brenda advanced. "You wouldn't play the harassment card, if it came to that? Seduce him and then blow the whistle to get him out of the way? That would be a terrible plan, Kim. It would be desperate, and unlike you."

Kim nodded. "In any case, I'm thinking I might have to get plastered before that meeting in the bar."

"You don't drink. You never drink."

"Exactly."

"Fine," Brenda said doubtfully. "But if it goes all haywire, please leave me the red shoes in your will for when this is all over, and the comfy chair by the window in your apartment."

Kim grabbed her purse and headed for the door. Brenda was right. Revenge wasn't like her. Not even remotely. However, if Chaz Monroe continued to play the intimidation card, and if he proved himself to be another unreliable male adversary, she'd have to find the strength to enact Plan C. Char his ass.

"Cover for me, Bren," she called over her shoulder. "I'm going shopping."

"May the force of Mata Hari be with you," Brenda called out conspiratorially as Kim headed for the door.

# Three

Chaz had pegged the bar scene perfectly. Young people were expensively turned out. Women in chic attire carried neon martinis and threw air kisses. At thirty-two and in a sports coat, he felt like their slightly out-of-it older brother, though women eyed him up and down with avid interest and unspoken invitations in their eyes.

Half of these people probably worked for him in some capacity or another and didn't yet recognize him by sight. By the end of the month, he would know each and every name on his payroll, and all ten of the building's janitors. Just now, however, he needed to remain incognito and observe the scene while he waited. For her.

He chose a table in a dark corner and sat on a stool with his back to the wall and his eyes on the door.

"Big Brother is watching you," he said beneath his breath.

He didn't really like chic bars where the young and the restless gathered to prance and preen. He preferred quiet corners in coffee shops where actual conversation could take place. The bar would likely be neutral territory for Kim, though. There'd be no battle lines here, away from official turf. Nor would there be any one-on-one private time that might get him into trouble.

He ordered a draft beer from an auburn-haired server in a tight black dress, who had a small tattoo on one sleek upper arm. He kept his attention on the doorway Kim would soon walk through, wanting to witness her entrance and observe her for a minute before she saw him.

He had spent the last hour trying not to imagine what she would be like in action, and he now wondered which of the guys surrounding him might have dated her and known her intimately. The thought made him uncomfortable, as did the image of some other guy tasting the heat of her hot pink mouth.

He did know one thing for sure. He had put way too much emphasis on their brief meeting, and had given McKinley far too much credit as a femme fatale. Not long now, and he'd find out how ridiculous his fantasies had been, because nobody liked a diva who ruled from within the confines of a short, tight skirt, and a lot of people in this building liked Kim.

His beer arrived, along with a phone number scribbled on a napkin. Chaz looked around. A pretty brunette at another table raised her glass and smiled at him.

He smiled back.

Pocketing the napkin, he took a swig from his long-necked bottle and refocused on the door.

*Business first.*

Several people entered in a group, but Kim wasn't among them. The noise decibel was rising quickly as the crowd swelled and empty glasses piled up. Chaz could barely hear himself think—which might have been a good thing in this instance, since thoughts turned to *her* again.

Would she work this crowd or ignore it?

Had someone else been waiting for her before this meeting? That *appointment?*

His stomach tightened when he thought about it. He was beginning to feel damp around the collar in spite of the cold shower.

With the bottle hoisted halfway to his mouth, Chaz suddenly paused, feeling Kim's presence before he actually saw her.

Then there she was, at last, the sight of her like a drop-kick to his underutilized libido.

Again.

For the third time that day, he absolutely could not take his eyes off her. Tonight, the reason was downright blatant. Kim McKinley was a carnal vision in an eye-popping red dress. Tight, short and silky, that dress pulsed with the word *sex*. Cut low enough at the neckline for a far too revealing peek at bare, glistening, ivory flesh, it caressed her body, hugging each curve.

*Diva with a red dress on...*

He stifled a chuckle as she moved through the crowd by the door like a tawny-haired hurricane. He wasn't the only person who stared.

She had let down her hair. Golden strands gleamed in the darkened room, floating an inch or two below her chin and giving the impression that she possessed a halo. But it was a fact that no angel would dare to dress like that.

Chaz's stomach twisted at the sight. But Kim wasn't alone. Another woman accompanied her, as dark as Kim was fair. Points went to him for inviting Brenda Chang, who hopefully might already have knocked some sense into Kim about her future job description.

Another good gulp of his draft seemed to settle him as Chaz waited to see if McKinley would come over, or if she would expect him to bend in her direction. Her beautiful features were set. She didn't smile.

When Kim finally sighted him with a gaze like a searchlight, Chaz did a quick head-shake and slapped his bottle down on the table. He stood up.

As she approached, his gaze traveled down her length, stopping at her ankles. She looked taller tonight because she was perched on dangerously high heels, the kind he'd imagined her wearing the first time he'd seen her. Shiny crimson stilettos.

Chaz whistled to himself. He couldn't help it.

Had she read his mind that afternoon?

*So you really do know how to make an entrance. Well, okay. You have my full attention.*

He raised his bottle in acknowledgment of her presence, and ditched the urge to clap his hands at the show she was providing, sure the sexy clothes were meant for some lucky bastard's sensory pleasure in taking them off. It was possible she had lied about not having a date.

"Mr. Monroe," she said in greeting.

"Ms. McKinley." Chaz gave her a nod.

The electrical current whizzing through the air between them from the distance of two feet felt strong enough to have burned the bar to the ground. He didn't imagine that. Their chemistry was undeniable, at least on his end.

Fine hairs at the nape of his neck were stirring. Fire roared through his muscles, causing a twitch. These reactions were a further indication of their instantaneous attraction, and also a hint about being so close to a sin-coated challenge.

"I've brought someone you should meet," she said in that seductive drawl. "This is Brenda Chang."

Chaz held out a hand to Brenda, who took it, though her eyes avoided his.

"I'm happy to meet you in person, Brenda," he said.

"Thanks for the invitation to join you," Brenda returned.

"I heard that you two work closely together, and that you're a good team," he said.

"Yes, that's true," Brenda agreed.

She was an attractive young woman with porcelain skin, dark eyes and a slender body encased in a tasteful blue suit.

Gesturing to the table, Chaz said, "Care to sit down?"

Would Wonder Woman act on any suggestion he made? Quite surprisingly, she did. She slid sideways onto a stool and crossed her legs, placing the heel of one dagger-sharp stiletto just inches from his right calf and making Chaz ponder the idea of what those heels would feel like if they were in bed together. It was a thought he had vowed not to have tonight.

"So," he began, once they all were in place around the little table. He avoided staring at the spot where Kim's shapely knee disappeared beneath the colorful silk. "Thanks for coming."

"Shall we get right to it?" she asked.

This, too, was unexpected. Chaz rallied with another nod.

"I believe you wanted to speak about the Christmas campaigns?" she said.

Brenda passed her pal a silent glance of interest.

"Yes," Chaz replied. "I've read the contract from front to back. But first, would you like something to drink?"

"I could use some Chardonnay," Brenda announced in a breathy outburst, smiling at him.

"Martini," Kim said.

"Oh, boy," Brenda muttered after hearing her friend's drink order. She flashed Chaz another pretty smile.

Of course Kim wanted a martini, the drink of choice for the young, pretty people these days. Still, Chaz, for reasons he didn't quite understand, had expected her order to be bottled water with a lemon wedge. He was a little disappointed to have been wrong about that as he flagged down the server.

"What kind of martini would you like?" he asked.

Oddly enough, the simple query seemed to stump her. She glanced to Brenda.

"You always like the appletinis here," Brenda prompted.

"Yes. That's what I'll have," Kim said. Turning to Chaz, she added, "Now, where were we?"

Was he wrong in his impression that she didn't know what an appletini was, and that there was something going on between Kim and Brenda that caused Brenda to show concern? He was pretty sure that Brenda had just fed Kim a line about the drink order.

"I'm aware of your rather unusual contract," he said. "What I'd like to do is ask politely that you ink it out. I'm hoping you can see this as a special favor to the agency and to our clients."

"Do you mean the clients who would like to continue working with me?" she asked, stressing her point of being well liked by those accounts.

Chaz shrugged. Kim's scarlet dress and her chilly vibe were at odds with each other, a dichotomy that did nothing to lessen the warmth searing through him each time she moved.

"A vice president has to oversee all accounts," he said.

"Yes, you do," she tossed back, emphasis on *you*.

"Being new, I'd like your help," he said. "Maybe we can start small on the help, and see how it goes?"

"I'm all ears, Mr. Monroe, as to what you might require." She did not glance at her watch, but added, "For the next ten minutes."

"It's Chaz. Please call me Chaz."

He was peripherally aware of how Kim's chest rose and fell laboriously with each new breath she took. Was that a sign of anger or anxiety? Outwardly, she looked calm enough. Cool, calm and collected. Yet she was electrically charged. He felt that charge pass through him. His heart beat a little faster.

"We've been asked to attend a special party for a potential new client, and I have volunteered to help make this an event. It's a very last-minute request, so with Ms. Chang already inundated, I'd need your help," he said.

He looked to Brenda, who passed the look on to Kim.

"Sorry." Kim carefully folded her hands around the stem of her glass when it arrived. "If you mean helping with something right now, that's impossible. I have the next two weeks off, starting tomorrow at noon."

"I'd be willing to double your holiday bonus for the extra time and effort," he said, applying a bit of preplanned pressure to see if money floated her boat. "We can talk about the clause afterward if you like."

Brenda took a sip of her wine and continued to gaze at Kim over the rim of her glass. Brenda appeared to be nervous about being in the middle of this conversation, and had started inching her glass sideways on the table as if she and the glass might make a quick getaway the first chance she got.

Good for her, for noticing where she wasn't needed. And to hell with the crowd. Chaz now wanted Kim all to himself. He wanted nothing more. They could hash this out, once and for all. If she remained stubborn, maybe they could arm wrestle a deal.

"I'm really sorry I can't help," Kim said, lush strands of gold brushing her face when she shook her head. "I've already made plans for my time off."

Chaz was actually starting to enjoy this game. He had always been good at chess. He did wonder, though, how far she'd go…and how far he'd go to stop her.

"Any way you might break those plans?" he asked.

"I'm pretty sure I can't at this late date."

"If I say please?"

She sat motionless for a minute, and then began to turn her glass in circles on the table without taking a drink. Chaz didn't fail to notice that she hadn't so much as placed her lips on the glass since it had arrived.

"As a favor to a potential client, then," Chaz said. "Not to me personally."

Another beat of time passed while he awaited her response.

"Didn't you just say that you read my contract?" she finally said with a subtle tone of disappointment underscoring her reply.

Chaz found himself fascinated with thoughts about how this would play out. He had said *please,* right? Surely she had to realize that this one decision could make or break the upward mobility of her career, at least with this agency.

He downed some beer and waited to see if she would explain herself.

"I truly am sorry," she said seconds later. "I'd be happy to help out any other time, with any other holiday. Really, I would help now if my situation were different."

"Different?" Chaz couldn't wait to hear this. If she was seriously involved in a relationship with some guy, and had *that* kind of plans for the next week, he'd have heard it from the people feeding him office gossip that afternoon. According to Alice, his agency bloodhound, Kim was pretty much a free agent in the serious relationship department.

"I'm…" she began.

"It's against her religion," Brenda said for her, and immediately flushed pink for having spoken out of turn.

Kim squirmed. He saw it. In the process, her left arm brushed his. Chaz's body responded with a jerk. The aftereffects of the surprise ignited a new and relatively irritating blaze of heat in his chest that robbed him of his next decent breath.

"Oh," he said. "That's what prevents you from working on all this holiday stuff?"

She recrossed her legs and blinked slowly. "Well…"

She didn't finish her excuse. A lovely flush crept up her neck, presenting a very seductive picture, for sure. The best he'd seen in a long time. But right then he wanted badly to throw her over his knee and give her a good spanking. *Bad little princess,* he'd say. *Why the white lies and the avoidance? Let's get right to the truth. You could do this if you wanted to.*

Or maybe he should just kiss her pouty mouth for all it was worth and see if that got a rise out of her. Maybe if they got that kiss out of the way, Kim might confess the real reasoning behind her ridiculous holiday reluctance.

On the other hand, she might slap his face and call it a night, and he'd be back to square one. Taking it further, she might take that walk, and take her clients with her.

Well, okay, there was a fine line between pushing her away and getting what he wanted, but he did owe her a shot at the title she coveted.

His inner musings on how this might go ceased abruptly when she leaned forward over the edge of the table. His eyes dipped to the sight of the dewy top of her rounded breasts and the fact that she wore nothing beneath the red dress. Nothing visible, anyway.

Although the sight doubled his heart rate, a thought occurred about this sudden closeness potentially being a purposeful move on her part to distract him, an enactment of the power of her all-too-obvious feminine wiles. Of which she had plenty.

Hell, maybe he just got turned on by the promise of a good fight. In his family, close as they were, fighting had become a sport.

The truth, though, was that he had grown tired of women who assumed they were owed something because of their looks. That aside, he had a short span of time to get this agency working better, and a Wonder Woman could help him do that.

Working this out would be the decent thing to do. The best outcome for everyone.

"Anyway, as I was saying, it's a special event," he continued. "If you'll hear me out, I'll explain."

She had no immediate reply to that, and continued to absently fondle the fragile stem of her glass in a way that he found extremely appealing.

At the same time, he was nearing his limit on patience. He noticed Brenda looking at him intently, and that look served to clear his mind.

"I'll find someone to help you," Kim finally offered. "I can find someone who will do a good job and is an ace at spur-of-the-moment stuff."

"Who would that person be?"

"Will you excuse me a minute?" Brenda broke in. "I have to, well, you know." Her exit was abrupt.

Kim didn't seem to notice her friend's departure. She didn't lean back or try to make her own escape.

"All right," she said. "I'll hear you out since I don't seem to have much choice in the matter, and then suggest somebody to help you. What is this special project?"

Chaz tried really hard not to grin. Kim had just given in, and an inch was better than nothing.

"It's a party. A Christmas party, and as much of an extravaganza as we can pull together this late. Nothing huge, really, and more indicative of a big family celebration. We'll need decorated trees, live music and a couple elves."

"Elves?" she repeated with a touch of sarcasm in her tone.

Chaz nodded. "Can't have Christmas without elves. Then we'll need packages. Large boxes, small boxes, all with big red bows. And snow."

"Snow?" Kim offered up an expression of surprise that overrode her former skepticism about elves.

"Sure. We can bring some snow inside a building, can't we? Aren't there snow machines? We can bring in some of the real stuff on trays and carts for the buffet table, as well as ice sculptures."

She winced, probably unwilling to tell him what an idiot he was for suggesting real snow inside a building. It likely cost her plenty to hold that chastisement in.

"We're not party planners," she said calmly. "You do know that we're a respected advertising agency?"

Chaz couldn't address that. He didn't dare. This was a test. A silly one, true, but he had to make it sound as if he needed her help. He couldn't say that it was his family's party he'd invade with all those Christmasy things if Kim actually agreed. In the meantime, he'd try to find out what irked her about the holiday stuff. He'd use all the holiday terms to push her buttons.

"Candy canes," he continued. "Mounds of them. Also anything and everything else that could make an indoor fantasy come true for the company and its top tier of stockholders."

McKinley's lush lashes closed over her eyes. Her hand stopped caressing the glass. She seemed to have stopped breathing.

"This must be a big deal," she said at length.

"Indeed, it's very big. For you."

McKinley's expression changed lightning fast. She sat upright on her stool, taking most of her deliciously woodsy scent with her.

Chaz's grin dissolved. Had he accidentally put the wrong spin on that last remark, making it sound sexual? Hell, he hadn't even thought about it, and sure as heck hadn't meant it that way.

"It's a potentially huge contract," he rushed to say, thinking that if she would merely agree, this would be over. One little "yes" and she'd be on her way to the metaphorical Oval Office. She just had to be willing to circumvent that stubborn mind-set and get down to business.

She didn't have to set one red-hot foot in his apartment. She didn't have to breathe in his goddamned ear. Those were daydreams. Man stuff. Wishful thinking. Most men were wired with those kinds of thoughts. All she had to do was cave on one little point, encapsulated by a single paragraph on paper.

But again, and to her credit, Kim didn't run away.

"Who is offering the contract?" she asked politely.

"I'm not at liberty to say. Not until you agree to help out."

"I did mention that I'm on vacation next week?"

"I'll give you a longer vacation at another time."

"I can't help you," she declared. But contrary to sounding smug about this persistent refusal, Chaz heard in her voice something else. Sorrow? Wishfulness? A silent desire that she didn't have to be so stubborn and inflexible?

He looked at her thoughtfully. "Are you really of a religion that shuns this holiday?"

She shook her head. "Irish. Completely. Three generations back."

"Ah." Chaz's breath caught in his throat as one of her hands rested lightly on top of his hand on the table, flesh to naked flesh, and cool from her grip on the martini glass.

The urge to tug at his collar returned.

"I'd like to be honest with you." As her eyes met his, Chaz couldn't help but feel as if he were drowning. The look in her eyes made the crowd around them disappear.

"I'd appreciate it if you would," he said, slightly shaken by the intimacy of her touch and her sudden change of expression. Truly, it wasn't a normal occurrence for him to be affected by the antics of a woman. He wasn't sex starved. He didn't need to count on Kim for those fantasies when the pretty brunette at the next table continuously looked his way.

"It would be better for me if you didn't pressure me into this," she told him in a carefully modulated tone that deepened her accent.

"Explain, and maybe I won't. I am human, you know."

When she frowned, the delicate skin around her eyes creased.

"I have a problem," she said.

Her fingers moved on his as if trying to stress a point he didn't see. Chaz found himself listening especially diligently for whatever excuse she'd come up with next. He could hardly wait to hear what she had to say.

She moistened her lips with the tip of her tongue, a provocative, erotic action.

"It's embarrassing to speak of, so I don't," she began. "If you were to fire me because of sharing this very personal confidence, I don't know what I'd do."

She hadn't removed her hand from his. His gaze lingered on her mouth.

"I have a problem with Christmas." As she spoke, earrings buried somewhere in her fair blond hair tinkled with a sound like stardust falling.

"It's not the holiday itself that bothers me," she went on. "An objection to the commercialism of Christmas would be funny in our line of business, wouldn't it?"

Kim's wan smile lifted the edges of her lips. "That's not the source of my problems."

"I'd sincerely like to know what is," Chaz said.

In another surprising move, she slid closer to him, inching her stool sideways and leaning in so that she didn't have to shout. With her mouth all but touching his right ear, she said, "Santa is my problem."

When Chaz turned his head, their lips almost met. He felt the soft exhalation of her breath. "Santa?" he echoed, his abs shuddering annoyingly beneath his shirt. "As in Santa Claus? You have a problem with Santa Claus?"

"Yes." Her reply was devastatingly breathy.

Was she making fun of him?

"How can Santa Claus be a problem?" he asked.

"I want him," she whispered.

He waited for the meaning of this to hit. Then he began to laugh. She wanted Santa? This was so much better than her shunning the holiday for religious reasons, or thinking Christmas too commercial as an advertising executive, that it came off as completely unique. Kim McKinley deserved a crown for this excuse.

She had put him on, of course, and she'd had him going for a minute. Her acting skills were applause-worthy. This was another point for her, well played.

But she didn't look so well, all of a sudden. Her smile had faded. Her face paled. The hazel eyes gazing into his were glazed and moist, very much as if she had just disclosed a terrible secret and was awaiting a dreaded response. As if she'd been serious.

And he had laughed.

Sobering, rallying quickly, he said, "I'm sorry. Please forgive me. I must have misunderstood your meaning. In what way do you want Santa Claus, exactly?"

"I..."

"Yes?"

"Well, you see, I..."

Her eyes held a pleading, haunted cast. She didn't want to explain herself, couldn't find the words. As he watched her, she began to look less like a mistress of fire, and more like a young, lost waif.

Chaz was moved by the change. Without thinking, he reached up to cup her face with his hands in an automatic reaction of empathy, sensing real trouble in her past. She stared into his eyes, and he stared back, groping for what was going on here, and what she might mean.

When her lips parted, they trembled enough that he could see the quakes. She wasn't acting or kidding around. Kim had been deadly serious about needing to shun what was going on with this holiday.

Wanting to ease the pain reflected in her eyes, and needing to fix what he had set in motion, Chaz pressed his mouth to hers before even knowing what had happened. When realization hit, he kept very still with his mouth resting lightly on hers as he sized up what he had just done.

Her lips were soft, slick and completely, heartbreakingly tender. Way better than anything he could have imagined. Light-years beyond better. But the biggest surprise of all was that he hadn't gotten close to her out of lust or the lingering effects of the dress and the shoes. It had been an unconscious need to comfort her, protect her.

He had just glimpsed something sad curled up in McKinley's core beneath the glamour and efficiency. He had wanted a confession, and instead had stifled that confession with a kiss.

He didn't move, draw back or try to explain. Neither did she. His pressure on her lips remained slight but steady, in a connection he had desired from the first time he'd seen her. He supposed she might scream when he let her go, and he completely deserved the slap he'd receive, though in this circumstance, his intentions had been honorable.

Her lips, her breath, her taste, fascinated him and moved him further, stirring emotions tucked inside. Strands of her blond hair tickled his cheek in a way that suddenly seemed right and completely natural. And since it was too late, anyway, and the damage had already been done, he added more pressure.

As the illicit kiss deepened, Kim's lips parted beneath his. She let a sigh escape and didn't pull away. The slap Chaz expected never came. Their bodies remained motionless, inches apart, as their breath and mouths explored the parameters of this very public forbidden kiss.

Her breath was enticingly hot, deliciously scented and as seductive as anything imaginable. Reeling from the sensations and spurred on by those seductions, Chaz dared to draw his tongue slowly along the corners of her mouth.

As he breathed her in, tasted her lipstick, felt the moistness of her tongue meeting his, she joined him in this unexpected faux pas.

For a minute, for Chaz, they were no longer employer and employee, or adversaries; only a man and a woman acting on a primal attraction that they had tried unsuccessfully to ignore. Giving in, ruled by feeling, Chaz tossed away all thoughts about the possible consequences of such a public display, and went for broke.

# Four

Kim gripped the table with both hands. She heard the sound of her glass tipping, rolling, and couldn't reach out to stop it from crashing to the floor. She was locked to her new boss in a battle of bodies and mouths and wills. In a bad way. A physical way.

And it was sublime.

It was…beyond words.

With her eyes closed, she could sense Chaz Monroe's body in relation to hers and knew it was too far away for the flames to be so hot and all-encompassing. After several seconds with her lips plastered to his, her hands left the table as if they had a mind of their own. She was only vaguely aware of curling her fingers into the front of his beautiful blue shirt.

He tasted like beer, desire and of plans gone south. They weren't supposed to be doing this, like this. They were enemies of a sort, which made their actions run contrary to everything she had planned. How could she actually like the kiss she was supposed to hold against him if the harassment case idea became necessary? And was that plan necessary now?

Then why didn't she run away?

She hardly thought of anything but Monroe's mouth, and the result had her floating in a sensory fog. The kiss seemed to go on forever. Some distant part of her mind warned that she had to get out of this situation. She had to get away right that instant. This kiss could prove her downfall as well as his.

Yet her breasts strained against the red silk, her nipples hard and aching. The dress seemed much too tight and restrictive. Between her legs, she quaked with a new awakening.

She wanted more than a kiss. Her body demanded more.

Damn. She really hated this guy!

As his tongue teased and taunted and his lips became more demanding, Kim struggled to think. She had to keep it together. Plans A and B had failed miserably in the very fact that they were a success, but she could still turn this around. She could use this. *Would* use this…as soon as he stopped doing whatever the hell he was doing that felt so good.

His tongue swept over her teeth and across her lower lip, urging more participation. She tore at his shirt, tugging him closer with treacherous fingers, seeking a way inside his clothes.

His warm hands remained on her face, holding her while she drowned in his essence, his heat and the intensity of what they were doing. Chaz Monroe really was the epitome of everything masculine and powerful, right down to his kissing talent. He didn't ravage her or threaten to overpower. The kiss had started off tender and exploratory, without being tentative, then quickly escalated.

These feelings were a first, and they were outrageous. She wanted Monroe to throw her on the table and slide his heated palms over her thighs. She had never felt this out of control, had never been attracted to a man in such a fierce, feral manner.

But other than his warm hands on her cheeks, he made no further move to touch her. No illicit fondling, nothing that would have earned him a shove and a sharp reprimand if she had been thinking properly.

Kissing was supposed to be like this, yet for her, never was. No man had ever moved her in this way, making her want to surrender her hard-won hold on control.

And just when she had started to weaken further, he

tugged lightly on her lower lip and withdrew. The pressure on her lips eased. He removed his hands from her face slowly, as if reluctant to do so, leaving chills in their wake.

He remained close. His eyes bored into hers questioningly, offering a hint of a new kind of understanding that was so foreign to Kim, she misread it as sympathy. He spoke from inches away.

"What about Santa? Exactly?"

She expected to see a flicker of amusement in his eyes. Her stomach seized up as she waited for it, wondering if Monroe had merely been proving a point about being an experienced playboy able to get whatever he wanted from his latest acquisition.

*Bastard!*

Her heart tanked. Her mouth formed a steely line. She had almost fallen for that kiss, and for him. She hadn't been the one to put a stop to it.

"Kim?" Monroe's tone was a silky caress with a startlingly direct link to her trembling lower regions.

"I'm sorry," she replied breathlessly. "I just can't."

The words were forced, pitched low, angry. Kim got to her feet. Her knees felt absurdly weak and unsupportive.

"Kim," Monroe said again, standing with her, using her first name as if the kiss had earned him the right to be familiar. "Help me here. Give me something."

"That's funny," she said. "I thought I just did."

It was too late for confessions and explanations. There would be no laughing this off as a simple mistake. Dread filled Kim, so heavy it made her stomach hurt. Following that came a round of embarrassment.

She had worn the dress and the shoes, and those things had worked their magic, just as Brenda had predicted they would. Going beyond distraction, they had seduced Monroe into unwarranted intimacy. And though she had liked that moment of intimacy, in the end, Monroe had successfully manipulated her. As her boss, he would continue to push for answers.

She steadied herself with a hand on the edge of the table. Telling the truth was out of the picture now for sure, as was remaining in Monroe's presence for one second longer.

The ridiculous harassment case idea wavered in front of her as if it were written in the air. They had made out in the bar, surrounded by people, some of which were her fellow employees. Hopefully, none of them had noticed that she hadn't shoved Monroe away, and also the fact that she could no longer breathe properly.

After a kiss like that, so completely mind-numbing and seductive, she saw no other way out of this mess but to play the damsel in distress in order to save her traitorous ruby-covered ass. She hated that; despised the thought. But Monroe was a master at games.

With the hazy lingering imprint of his mouth on hers, Kim lifted a hand. She slapped Monroe across the face, hard, and said loudly enough for others to hear, "What were you thinking, Mr. Monroe? That I'd jump at the chance to bed my boss?"

Pivoting gracefully on her absurdly expensive shoes, she headed for the door, feeling the burn of Monroe's inquisitive gaze on her back and thinking that if she'd wanted to cry in frustration before, she had just taken it to a whole new level.

Shell-shocked, and beginning to get a bad feeling about what had just happened, Chaz smiled at the people at the next table and shrugged his shoulders. He couldn't quite believe this, though. He'd been completely helpless in resisting Kim McKinley. Once again, his plan had backfired.

He had locked lips with her. In public.

And he knew what that meant.

Waiting out several agonizing seconds before throwing

down cash for the drinks, he started after her, deciding that he wouldn't apologize if he caught up with her, since she had provoked that damn lip-lock.

That dress…

Those shoes…

The sudden waifish expression in her eyes.

There was no time like the present to get to the bottom of this charade and find out what Kim had up her sleeve. Certainly she had something up there.

He had taken the bait in what might have been a ploy to catch him off guard. Possibly a public seduction had been her goal all along. If so, this made McKinley a real master at manipulation.

He had believed, with his mouth on hers, and with her throaty moan of encouragement, that she wanted closeness as much as he did. That she enjoyed the kiss as much as he had.

Bottom line—he had believed her. He'd fallen victim to the flash of pain in her eyes and the acceptance of her lush mouth. He thought those things were real, as was the sorrow that had overtaken her saucy demeanor. He'd been sure the real Kim McKinley was facing him for the first time.

And she had played him?

What a sucker he'd been. Only one reason came to mind for an objective like hers—either the threat of a harassment case against him, or out-and-out blackmail. *A kiss for a clause.*

He didn't like his new title, which was Chaz Monroe, fool. People in the bar were looking at him. The brunette who had handed over her phone number winked knowingly.

Did Kim have any earthly idea what he'd like to do to her, now that he knew the score?

How could he have been so completely wrong? Because he would have sworn, testifying with one hand in the air and another on the Bible, that she had kissed him back and meant it.

Oh yes, she was good. Damn good. It had been a great performance. Perfect, actually.

"But it isn't over," Chaz said through gritted teeth as he moved through the crowd.

Kim strode past the bar's doorway and into the corridor beyond that led to the building's marble lobby. When she reached the bank of elevators, she punched a button with her palm and stamped her feet a couple of times in disgust. The wrong plan had worked. She felt terrible, sick.

All that evocative talk had done her in. Snow. Elves. Presents and candy canes. She hated the slinky red dress and the shoes she couldn't return.

The fact that she'd almost blurted out the truth about her family simply added fuel to the fire of an already demented situation. Now there was no going back. She'd have to nail Monroe to the wall by using that very public mistake if he continued to bug her about the contract.

To hell with Chaz Monroe for making her feel guilty about having to force her to use bribery and revenge to get him off her back. She cursed him for bringing up her dark past and causing her to become someone else, someone who would do such a thing for their own personal gain.

Darkness bubbled up inside her, coating her insides.

Once upon a time, she had wanted to trust a man for his good and magical qualities. She had wished hard for Santa Claus to bring her father back. On each anniversary of her father's exit, she had prayed for something to stop her mother's crying jags and all those days when her mom couldn't get out of bed.

She had secretly written to Santa once, and mailed the letter. But Santa hadn't bothered to respond or grant her that wish. Her father never returned, and her mother's depression got progressively worse until relatives had threatened to take Kim away.

The emptiness in her past was riddled with fear and loneliness and a young girl's angst. Her mother's rants and monologues had followed Kim everywhere, and guilt had made her stay close. Her mother didn't need another disappointment; couldn't have withstood her daughter leaving, too.

There had been no escape until college, and even there, while testing her wings, guilt had been part of Kim's existence. She had fled some of that darkness, while her mother had not. She was okay, and her mother stayed sick.

Tonight that sickness had become hers. She had become a player, against her will, as if her mother had risen from the grave to goad her on. She had been willing to hurt someone, a man, so that her secrets could go on being secrets, and her hurt stayed tucked inside. She had wanted to trust, and had been shot down.

"Kim?"

The voice was close, deep and too familiar for comfort. A wave of chills pierced Kim's red dress. The elevator was too damn slow, and she hadn't expected Monroe to follow her.

*Now what?*

Wobbling on her weakened knees, Kim whirled to face Monroe in all his gorgeous male beauty. The persistent bastard wasn't going to let her off the hook, but he wouldn't touch her again if he knew what was good for him.

He leaned toward her before she could voice a protest, and placed both hands on the wall beside her. It took him several seconds to speak.

"There's no need to run away." His tone seemed too calm for the expression on his face. He pinned her in place, within the cage of his arms, as if knowing she'd bolt at the first opportunity. The front of his shirt showed creases from where she had greedily tugged at it in a moment of blissful mindlessness.

Kim didn't reply. She could not think of one appropriate word to say.

"I really don't see the need for an all-out war, or whatever you imagine this is," he said. "I asked to meet in good faith to discuss the problems facing us. I was trying to find a way out of this mess."

Kim tried to hit the elevator button with her elbow. Though there'd likely be a hint of snow on the ground outside tonight, the corridor felt stiflingly warm. Part of that heat came from Monroe, who acted as if he knew exactly what she had done, and what the outcome had to be. *Clever man.*

"I believed we could work something out," he said. "For a minute back there, I thought you might honestly want to."

She had to fight for a breath. Monroe's closeness was a reminder of how far she had strayed. That kiss, in public, would be career doom for her if rumor of it got around. She wasn't the one with the VP spot. He was.

She tried to touch her lips, to wipe away the feeling of him, but couldn't raise her arms. Monroe's inferno pummeled at her, overheating her from the inside out, rendering her excuses for her behavior useless.

"I tried to explain," she managed to say.

Maybe he hadn't gotten the picture, after all, about the blackmail. His mouth lurked a few millimeters away from hers. Dangerously close.

"But you didn't explain. Not really," he said. "None of that was the truth, right?"

"More than you know."

"There's still time to explain, Kim."

She shook her head.

"I wasn't the only one who wanted that kiss," Monroe remarked. "And it wasn't planned."

"How dare you presume to know what I want?"

"Well, at least one of us is honest. I'll admit that it wasn't the goal of tonight's discussion, but I will also confess that I liked it. I liked it a lot."

"It was business suicide for me, and you know it."

"So, you'll use the kiss against me?"

"Do I have a choice?"

"Well, if it's a lawsuit you want, we might as well make the best of it. There's no need to slap me this time. What good would it do if no one is watching?"

Each time Kim inhaled, his shirt rubbed against the red silk of her dress, sending pangs of longing through places she hadn't focused on in a long time. The closer he got, the more of his disarming scent she breathed in.

She wanted that kiss his lips were promising. Another kiss. A better one, if there was such a thing, especially given that no one, as he said, was there to witness it.

With that thought, Kim knew she was screwed. Chaz Monroe wasn't merely an intelligent bastard, his actions were highly suspicious. Was he a man ruled by what was in his pants, or did he have some nebulous plan of his own to humble her with?

When his mouth brushed across her right temple, Kim squirmed and glanced up to meet the directness of his gaze. She absorbed a jarring jolt of longing for the closeness she had to repel. Monroe was her boss. No one in the company could condone a relationship with him that might eventually lead to the promotion she already deserved. Rumors were a plague in business. If she were to get a promotion in the near future, some would now say she had slept her way to the top.

Several coworkers had witnessed what happened in the bar. Whereas it might have gone unnoticed if she'd kept quiet, in a moment of panic she had idiotically made sure it hadn't gone unnoticed. Plan C had been set in motion.

*Damn him. Damn you, Monroe.*

"Why can't you leave me alone?" she demanded.

His breath stirred her hair. "Obviously, that contract involves personal issues for you that I hadn't anticipated."

"Bravo for concluding that."

"I have no way of knowing what those issues are unless you tell me about them."

"They aren't your business. Not something so personal. Leave it, Monroe. I'm asking you to let it go."

"Or what? A bit of blackmail will back your request up?" He sighed. "I'm concerned, that's all. Neither of us has to be those people in the bar. We can be friends if you'd prefer that. I'm actually a good listener. We could go someplace quiet and talk things over."

"Like your apartment?"

He shook his head.

"But you'd like to take me to your apartment," she said.

"What fool wouldn't? But that's not the point here."

"I've asked you to back off."

He touched the cheek she had slapped. "Right. I got that."

"And you refuse to listen," Kim said.

"I don't tend to take no for an answer when a moment like the one in the bar told me otherwise."

"Then we can finish this tomorrow," Kim said. "After we've thought it over and had some distance."

"I'm fairly certain we should finish this now," Monroe countered. "I'd really like to know what upsets you. I thought you were going to cry."

His gaze was volcanic. He had nice eyes. Great eyes. Light blue, with flecks of gold. Those eyes wouldn't miss much, if anything. He would see her cave. Right then, his gaze sparkled with a need to understand what she had been thinking, beyond the possibility of blackmail. Or else maybe he just wanted to know more about the terms of their deal.

Letting Monroe strike a nerve is what had gotten her into this mess. He was too handsome, and too willing to get to know her better. Men like him often used women, her mother had preached. If you gave them your secrets, they'd betray those secrets at the drop of a hat. If you gave them your love, they'd easily destroy it.

Kim wanted desperately to stop hearing her mother's voice. She would have covered her ears if Monroe had let her.

"If you're going to fire me for slapping you, go ahead," she said a bit too breathlessly for the sternness she had been aiming for. "There's no need for us to further humiliate each other."

"Fire you? Humiliate you? I wanted to meet with you to avoid those things."

"Well, you didn't do a decent job of reaching that objective. Now you do want to fire me, right? You'll have to, unless I protect myself?"

"That was never the idea, Kim. You'll have to believe me."

"Then why can't you leave me alone? We were doing fine here until you arrived."

"Fine? This company was sliding, whether or not you knew about the bottom line. It was in serious decline. I came here to help the agency out of that decline. The company's success means a lot to me because I have a stake in it. I need everyone to work, including you. If you're one of the best people here, your help is needed in all areas."

"I've been doing more than my share."

"I know that, and yet I need more. I'd ask you to do things you don't necessarily want to do because the company requires it right now, and for no other reason."

"Not because you want to kiss me again?"

"Yes, damn it. I want to kiss you. But believe it or not, I do have some control."

He leaned closer as he spoke, so that Kim felt every muscle in his body from his shoulders to his thighs, and everywhere in between. Yet his mouth drew her focus: the sensuous, talented mouth that had nearly done her in.

"It's going to be yes or no," Monroe said. "You have it within your power to upgrade, maybe even to upper management someday. All you have to do is what I ask, or explain why you can't."

Kim shut her eyes.

"Look, Kim. Do this one thing for me, and we'll reevaluate your position here."

Kim stopped shaking just as she realized she was shaking. Like the last VP, Monroe was promising her the moon when he had no real capacity for giving it to her. He was the vice president. The only way for her to take over that job was for him to leave it.

"I'd like you to leave me alone," she repeated.

"The company needs you."

"Yes. With your body pressed against mine in a public hallway, I can feel how badly you need me."

That did it. Enough was enough. No more squirming. No more playing around. Chaz Monroe had finally done it. He had just buried himself.

Smiling grimly, Kim reached into the purse hanging at her side. She pushed Monroe away and drew out the small tape recorder she kept there. With a precise movement of her finger, she clicked the gadget off.

He glanced at her in surprise, then looked down at what she held in her hand as if not quite believing what he was seeing.

"My lawyer will be talking to your lawyer in the morning if there is any further mention of my contract," Kim said, slipping out from beneath his arm. "You have heard of sexual harassment, being number-one boss man and all?"

He was staring at her as though he'd just felt the arrow of doom pierce his heart dead-on, and also as if he had been betrayed. His arms dropped to his sides. His expression smoothed into something unreadable.

The elevator pinged as the door rolled open. Kim walked inside and turned, wearing a smile she had to struggle to maintain. Her insides were in knots. Both hands were shaking. She hid her sadness and the urge to throw the recorder at Monroe. She felt like sinking to the ground.

He just stood there. He didn't look angry, only disappointed. He had been bushwhacked, broadsided. Did he fear what would happen to him if this conversation were to fall into the wrong hands? Did he now fear for his job?

Monroe had a casting couch, pure and simple, and she'd nearly been flat out on top of it. So what if she had liked the kiss and his hard body pressed to hers? It was best not to think about those things now. The guy, gorgeous as he was, charming as he could be, shouldn't have taken such liberties. The vice president should have known better.

With a stern bite to her lower lip, Kim used her purse to snap the button inside the elevator that would close this case once and for all. Was she proud of how she'd accomplished this? *No.* Happy about it? *Absolutely not.* She felt dirty. Yet she had remembered the recorder at the last minute and done what had to be done.

Monroe wouldn't fight her. Nothing good ever came of a lawsuit. So, the hope she maintained right that minute was that he would realize this and stop bothering her to change the terms of her contract. Life as usual would be the result.

The dark clouds she had been trying so hard to shake off drifted over her. She pictured her mother smiling. In reaction, Kim felt her face blanch. She swayed on her feet, truly hating what she had done and the memories that wouldn't stop invading her mind, all because of her mother's far-reaching influence.

This night was over, and it was too late to take anything back. She had made her bed, but at least Monroe wasn't in it.

"Good night," she said to him with a catch in her throat.

He stood in the corridor, motionless, his eyes on her as the elevator doors finally closed.

# Five

*Well, well...*

Kim had called his bluff. She thought she'd done pretty well in this game, and he had to hand it to her. She'd hung in there and had been fairly creative about it. Still, the result was a disappointment. He hadn't figured she would go so far in the wrong direction.

As the elevator doors closed between them, Chaz shrugged his shoulders. He knew that Kim had to be feeling a little guilty after hearing him state his case. She wasn't dense. The telling detail about her current state of mind was that aside from the tape recorder, she hadn't slapped him again.

Hearing the clink of rapidly approaching heels on the marble floor, Chaz turned and said, "That wasn't remotely close to what we had discussed."

Brenda Chang strode up to him wearing a frown. "I don't feel very well. I feel like I've just stabbed my best friend in the back because—oh wait—*I have.*"

"You left us alone out of the goodness of your heart," he pointed out.

"Yes, but you didn't pay me enough to betray her."

"I didn't pay you anything at all."

"That's what I mean."

"I had to try to reach her. I did try." Chaz shook his head, eyeing the elevator.

"You have no idea how much she'd like to capitulate. She's just not ready," Brenda said.

"There's no way to help with that? You won't tell me what her problem is?"

"Not for love or money. Wild horses couldn't drag Kim's secrets from me without her permission."

Chaz ventured another lingering look at the elevator.

Brenda's voice sounded small. "What next?"

"My hands are tied. She wants to be left alone."

"You already knew that."

Chaz shot her a look that indicated quite clearly that he wasn't in the mood to prolong this discussion.

"All right," Brenda said. "But you'd better turn out to be a good guy, that's all I can say, or you'll have problems added onto problems. That's a promise."

Chaz leaned back to read the numbers on the elevator panel above the door. "If she's going back to the office, will she stay up there long?"

Brenda shrugged.

"Does she need your shoulder to lean on?" he asked.

"I doubt it. Besides, she'll probably get out one floor up and use the stairs to leave the building, knowing she'd get past you that way."

Brenda's eyes widened when she realized she'd said too much.

"That shrewd, eh?" he asked.

She blew out a sigh. "Every woman knows how to do this, Monroe. Avoidance is coded into in our genes."

"So what will she do after that?"

"Simmer awhile, most likely, and then start thinking."

"She doesn't really have a case you know," he said. "There's no one to remove me or waggle a finger over a kiss."

Brenda nodded. "I know that, and who you really are. You might have changed your name if being undercover here is your game, because I just looked your family up online. Kim doesn't know yet because I didn't get to it until now."

"You looked me up?"

"The internet is a marvelous thing," Brenda said. "Your family's business dealings are plastered all over it."

"Then you know why I'm here?"

"Yep."

"You'll tell her?"

"I would have already, if you hadn't followed her to this hallway. Just so you know, friends don't usually allow each other to do anything they might regret."

"When she knows about me, and without her little blackmail scheme getting her the office she wants, will she leave the company?"

"I wouldn't put it past her. What would you do, in her place, if you found out that the man you were going to resort to blackmailing was in fact the owner of the agency?"

"I'd take the damn Christmas gig and get on with it," Chaz said.

"Yes, well you have millions of dollars to fall back on, and no female hormones. Kim has a tiny apartment she can barely afford as it is, close by because she's here working most of the time."

Chaz gave her a sober sideways glance. "Point taken."

"Is it?" Brenda countered.

"Quite."

"She's not putting you on, you know. She has been dealing with holiday stuff for years. Very real issues. Serious setbacks."

Chaz looked again to the elevator, which had indeed stopped two floors up. He then glanced to the revolving doors leading to the street. "I don't suppose you'll tell me where her apartment is?"

"The name is Chang, not Judas."

"I want to keep her, but I'm running out of options, Brenda. I'd like to tell her about my real position here, myself, before she does anything stupid."

"So you'll show up on her doorstep?"

"Do you have a better idea?"

"I think that might be going beyond the call of duty. Unless there's another reason you want to keep her here, other than her ability to work her tail off."

Chaz thought that over, deciding that Brenda was right. He was letting an employee dictate his actions, actions that might appear as desperate. As for a reason for wanting to keep Kim, beyond chaining her to her desk...his body had made it pretty clear that he was interested in more than her work ethic. The intensity of their attraction that had led to the kiss couldn't be ignored, and hadn't lessened one bit.

It was a double-edged sword. If he went out of his way to keep her at the agency, his actions tonight might hurt her reputation. If she walked out, taking those big clients with her, the agency might tank.

This was an impossible situation that he had to try to put right.

"You're right," he said to Brenda. "She has to decide for herself, without further interference, what she will do next. Feelings have no place here."

Brenda thought that over with her head tilted to the side. She searched his face. "Feelings, huh?"

He shrugged.

She sighed loudly and opened her purse. Removing a piece of paper and a pen, she scribbled something and handed the paper over.

"If you tell her I gave this to you, I'll tell her you lied. Three guesses as to whom she will believe."

After a hesitation, she handed him something else. It was a tiny tape recorder just like the one Kim had used to record their conversation.

Chaz glanced at her questioningly.

"I taped something in case Kim and I needed a laugh later," Brenda said. "You might want to listen to the tape before finding her. It might help with that lawsuit business and save everyone some serious damage."

Chaz pocketed the recorder. "Does this mean you'll trust me to set things straight?"

"Hell, no. It's bribery for you to leave me out of what-ever happens from this point on."

Chaz decided right then that he really did like Brenda Chang.

"Will she shoot me if I show up at her place?" he asked.

"I would."

He smiled. "I suppose following her seems desperate."

"Completely."

"Okay then, wish me luck."

"Boss, you are so going to need it," Brenda declared as Chaz headed for the street.

Kim's feet were killing her. Stilettos required a lot of downtime and motionless posing, not trotting down New York sidewalks, contrary to what TV shows might have everyone think. The shoes were impossible, especially on the icy sidewalk.

She waved down an oncoming taxi, waited until it stopped, then ran in front of it to cross the road, assured of not getting hit when the taxi blocked traffic. The driver grumbled, and might have extended one finger in a rude gesture. She didn't wait to see.

Thankfully, her apartment was around the corner from the agency, at the end of the block. Though close in terms of actual distance, she'd still have to soak her feet when she got there, and also work with her fractured ego.

The heels made sharp pecking sounds on the sidewalk as she threaded her way between other pedestrians. She'd left the office without her coat, and the red dress garnered a few stares and catcalls from men she passed.

"Imbeciles." What kind of man gave a woman a whistle on the street that she could hear?

She was shivering, but she'd had to get out of the agency building. Since Monroe had followed her into the hallway, he might have continued to the office. If he had pushed his way into the elevator with her, filling the tiny, confined space with his musky, masculine maleness, there was no way to predict what might have happened. Plus, there were cameras.

Any more time spent in Chaz Monroe's sight would be bad, and how much worse could she feel?

She walked with her gaze lowered, having set up her mental block against the windows in the stores she passed that were decorated with December finery. Some of them presented animated holiday scenes. Others showcased giant trees decorated with everything under the sun that could fit on a branch. It was especially important she didn't view these things in entirety; not after dealing with Monroe.

She was already on edge.

With great relief, she made it down the block without seeing a single Santa suit on a street corner—a sight that would not only have filled her with the old regrets, but also reminded her of what she had told Monroe.

She wanted Santa....

Yes, she had told him that.

Well, okay. So she had been impulsive enough to use Brenda's ridiculous excuse in a moment of panic and extreme need. Therefore, could she really blame Monroe for thinking her an idiot?

She wanted Santa. *Jeez...*

Feeling sicker, Kim rushed on. She nodded to the doorman of her building and whisked by without the usual benign chitchat. Six floors up and down one long hallway, and she was home free. No one had followed her. No pink slip waited on the floor by her door.

Kim stood with her back to the wood as the door closed behind her, only then allowing herself a lungful of air. She really did feel sick. Tonight she had been possessed by her mother's teachings. She'd been set back a few years with the flick of a tape recorder switch.

"There's no going back. No taking it back," she muttered.

The guilt tripled with her second breath of air. Even from the small front room, not much larger than her cubicle at work, she smelled the cookies she had dared to bake the night before.

Christmas cookies.

Her first disloyal batch.

The damn cookies might have been some kind of terrible omen. She had looked up the recipe in secret, and baked them as her first baby step toward freedom. Now her new boss had whispered fantastical things in her ear without realizing how much she'd love to participate in Christmas festivities, and how much it hurt to think of actually doing so.

*Elves. Snow. Packages in red ribbons.* She might have given her right index fingernail to join in everything going on around her, and had been slowly inching in that direction.

Then she kissed Chaz Monroe.

She hung her head. Her apartment smelled like a sugar factory. Worse yet, she wanted her place to smell like *him*. Like Monroe, companionship, sex, holiday glitter and all the other things her mother had shunned so harshly. You'd think she'd know better. Someone looking in on her life might expect her to just wipe the slate clean and start over, now that her mother was no longer in the picture. Who from the outside would understand?

If she tossed the cookies, would things change? If she marched into the kitchen and got rid of the little doughy stars and trees, would time reset itself backward so that she'd have another chance to get things right?

Monroe was a jerk. He had to be. Because if he wasn't, then she was.

Tossing her purse to the floor, Kim staggered to the couch and threw herself onto it, face-first, listening to the side seam in her tight red dress tear.

Chaz glanced at the paper, then up at the tall brick building. This was it. McKinley lived here, and he was going to trespass on her space and privacy because tonight he felt greedy. He wanted a showdown to get this over with once and for all.

She lived in a place that was a lot like his on the outside. He didn't know her well enough to gauge her decorating skills, but figured martini glasses wouldn't be one of her prominent fixtures.

In truth, he didn't really know Kim at all and was relying on the concept of animal attraction to nudge him into doing what he'd never done before—plead his case a second time.

He offered a curt but friendly nod to the doorman and went inside. The doorman picked up the lobby phone and dialed apartment 612.

"Yes?" she answered after a couple of rings.

The doorman spoke briefly, then handed the phone over.

Hearing Kim's voice left him temporarily tongue-tied, something so unlike him that he almost hung up. He thought about the napkin with the brunette's number on it crumpled up in his pocket. Calling that number might have taken his mind off Kim McKinley for a few hours.

So, the fact that he was standing here meant he was either acting like a madman, or a man possessed. Maybe even like a sore loser refusing to give up on the outcome he wanted. Those flaws made him see red. And in the center of that puddle of red was Miss Kim McKinley, the cause of all this.

"Delivery for Kim McKinley, advertising queen," Chaz said to her over the line, managing to keep his voice neutral. "I can't be sure, but from the feel of the package, I think it contains an apology."

A short span of silence followed his remark. His heart beat faster. What was he doing here, anyway? Had he just uttered the word *apology?*

"This only adds to the harassment, you know," she eventually said. "I believe stalking might be a felony."

"Yes, well, what's one more year behind bars when there's so much at stake?"

"None of this is funny, Monroe."

"No, it isn't. At least we agree on something."

"You can't come up."

"Then maybe you'll come down."

"Sorry."

"Are you sorry?"

After another hesitation, she said, "No."

"Not very convincing," Chaz remarked. "It's that gap between what you say and what you don't say that keeps me wondering what you might really be thinking."

More silence. A full twenty seconds, by his calculation. Chaz lowered the phone to keep her from hearing his growl of disappointment, then thought better of it. With the phone so close to his heart, she might be able to hear how fast it raced. She'd know something was up.

"You just don't get the picture," she accused. "I don't know you at all."

"You know me well enough to want to prosecute me for minor indiscretions. Also, I did say I'm willing to take on an added year in the slammer if you think I need it after we hash this out."

"Can I have that in writing? About the slammer?"

"I'm fresh out of pens."

"How convenient."

"You do have a tape recorder, though," he reminded her. "It's possible you're using it now."

Silence.

"You don't know how persistent I can be, Kim. Lawsuit or not, blackmail or whatever, I still have to take care of business while the fate of that business rests in my hands. Don't you have a sympathetic bone in your body? Can't you put yourself in my place?"

"I was supposed to be in your place."

"Water under the bridge, Kim. How long can you hold that against me?"

Another silence ensued. Chaz held his breath.

"Let me speak to Sam," she said.

"Sam?"

"The doorman. He'll come if you call."

Chaz called out to the man, and he ambled over and took the phone.

"Yep," Sam said to the receiver, nodding. "Yep. I certainly will, Miss McKinley." Then Sam hung up the phone.

"What did she say?" Chaz asked.

"I'm to take something as collateral, then send you up."

"Excuse me?"

"Miss McKinley wants me to hold something as ransom, in order for you to visit her apartment. You can pick that item up again when you come back downstairs. I have instructions to call the police if you don't pick it up within the hour."

"Like what?" Chaz said. "My wallet?"

"The value of that as collateral depends on what's in it," Sam said without missing a beat.

"Who do I call if I come back and you're not here with my wallet?" Chaz asked.

Sam looked dramatically aghast at the suggestion. "I

have a drawer right here, and I'll lock it up, minus whatever you see fit to give me for keeping it safe. If you prefer,
I can give the wallet to a neutral third party."

"What kind of doorman are you?"

Sam held out his hand, palm up. "The kind that cares
about his wards."

Chaz fished for his wallet, took out a wad of cash and
his credit cards, then handed a twenty-dollar bill and the
wallet to McKinley's private watchdog.

He held up the rest of the cash. "Just in case I have to buy
off anyone else between here and her apartment."

Sam grinned and pressed the elevator button for him.
"Apartment 612. Have a nice night."

The elevator was slow and bumpy, but Chaz stepped
out on the sixth floor. He found number 612 a few doors
down, its oiled wood glowing in the light from the wall
sconce beside it.

As he waited to knock, he pondered further what Kim's
home would be like, half dreading finding out. Personalities
were reflected in a person's surroundings. If she preferred
chintz chairs, mounds of pillows and draperies with fringe,
he wasn't sure what he'd do. Run away, maybe. After all,
he didn't want to marry McKinley. He just wanted to…

Well, he wanted to…

*God, would she have a cat?*

He'd be a dog guy, himself, if he had any time or space
for pets.

And it was perfectly clear that what he was doing with
all this ridiculous speculation was trying to talk himself out
of this next meeting with her after getting this far.

Fingering the tape recorder in his pocket, he knocked
softly.

"Yes?" she called out.

"Monroe. Not completely broke, I might add, because

Sam showed a little mercy. I think he recognized your real intention, which was to put me in my place."

"Say what you wanted to say and then go away."

"From here, with the door between us? What would the neighbors think?"

The door opened a crack. Kim's face appeared behind a stretched brass chain. "Go away, Monroe. We have nothing further to say to each other tonight."

"Then why did you let me come up?"

"To tell you that to your face."

He noticed right away that she looked smaller. She had ditched the red shoes, but still wore the red dress that glowed like liquefied lava in the light from the sconce.

"If I let you in," she added, "it might ruin my lawsuit. So why are you here?"

"You're a challenge I have to take up."

"Is that supposed to be a compliment, or are you merely the type of person that needs to win at all cost?"

"Winning isn't everything," he countered. "The need to understand you is why I'm here."

"What part of *none of your business* don't you get?"

"You kissed me," he said, wondering why he'd brought that up again. He'd kissed other women, for heaven's sake.

"So?" she said.

"Was it me or the game you might be playing that made you do it?"

She closed the door. He heard it seal tight.

"Would you prefer I spoke about holiday clauses here? How about if I mention Santa, and how you made that sound in the bar?"

The door opened again, not quite as widely, showing off Kim's exquisitely creased expression. "That's not funny."

Chaz shrugged. "What more have I got to lose?"

"How about your job?"

"Okay, Kim. But remember, you forced me to do this."

From his pocket, Chaz pulled out the tape recorder Brenda had handed him. He had listened to it on the way over, and bookmarked a starting point in case of just such an instance as this, figuring Brenda wouldn't have handed the tape over if it wasn't something useful to his cause.

He hit Play. Brenda's voice came from the tiny speaker.

*Tell me about it. But first you have to dish about whether Monroe really does have a nice ass. You didn't think he was hot? That's the word going around. H-o-t, as in fan yourself.*

*Yeah? Did you hear anything about the man being an arrogant idiot?*

*No. My sources might have left that part out.*

*I don't actually care about the nice ass part, Bren, preferring not to notice an area that I won't be kissing.*

*Don't be absurd, Kim. No one expects you to kiss anyone's backside. It isn't professional. What happened?*

*I'll have to start over somewhere else, that's what. Monroe won't let me off the hook. He expects me to explain everything. He'll expect me to cave.*

As Chaz fast-forwarded slightly, he said, "I don't think Brenda knew she was recording that. She had been making notes for herself on a project."

He held the recorder up and pressed Play again.

*If you don't want to tell Monroe the truth, you have about an hour to formulate a reason he'll accept in lieu of the truth. Fabricating illusions is what we do on a daily basis, right? We make people want to buy things.*

Chaz pocketed the recorder. "Then there was something about shoes and therapy and a Santa fetish."

Kim stared at him through the crack.

"Also, I believe that seducing me was mentioned, which might tend to negate that harassment suit and the blackmail you might have planned on using to get me to back down."

Kim looked very pale, in stark contrast to her red dress.

"So, there is no Santa fetish?" he asked. "You made that up?"

Now she looked sick, and he felt bad. But he wanted her to let him in. He needed to get that far for reasons he did not want to contemplate.

"Why are you here?" she asked. "What do you want?"

"You and I tending to that Christmas party by working together."

"You have no idea what you're asking."

"That's the point. I want to understand. Until you can help me do that, we're back to square one."

"No. We're back to you filling my place at the agency, because I'm out of there as of right now."

Chaz shook his head. "Now you're being stubborn. No one wants you to go, myself included. I've come here personally to tell you so, at much risk to my ego, I might add. Can't that constitute a win on your part if you're keeping score?"

She paled further. Possibly she wasn't used to direct confrontations.

He held up the recorder. "How about if you get yours and we toss them both out the window?"

"We're six floors up."

"There's little chance of them surviving the fall, right?"

"They might hit somebody. Maybe Sam."

Chaz nodded thoughtfully. "Okay. You're right. It would probably be simpler if we exchanged tapes. Then no one would have the goods on anyone else."

"This is ridiculous," she said. "What do you want?"

"Talk and a holiday party," he said. "That's all I ask."

"Okay."

"Okay?" he repeated, surprised by her reply.

"When is this damn party?" she asked.

"In a week or so."

"That's only a few days before…"

"Christmas," Chaz supplied.

She looked hesitant. "I can make some calls."

"You will do this personally, Kim?"

"Yes."

"Thank you." Chaz wasn't sure about feeling relieved, because winning this round wasn't as satisfying as it should have been. Kim was going to pass the test after being shoved into it, but he might have pushed her too far. Her sudden acceptance reflected that. He had, he supposed, lost by winning, and he experienced an immediate pang of regret.

"It's the last thing I'll do for you," she said, confirming his diagnosis of the situation.

Chaz wanted to let it go at that. At the same time, he desired to tell her she really didn't have to work on the ridiculous and imaginary project, and that he was sorry for putting her through this. Breaking her would have hurt both of them, and that realization came as a further surprise, because he found that he liked Kim exactly the way she was.

"I know it might be true that you'll decide to leave, but I'm counting on convincing you otherwise. I am sorry we had to meet like this," he said.

How serious he had grown in saying what he truly meant. Chaz fought a strange impulse to break the little chain keeping them apart and wrap his arms around the pale version of McKinley facing him. Again, his instinct was to protect her, comfort her, though he had no idea why. She was Wonder Woman, after all.

*Okay.* Backtracking, maybe he did know why he wanted to hold her. He had started to like her more than was appropriate, in spite of her stunt in the bar.

"Where is the party?" Her voice sounded dry. Her accent was pronounced, and no less sultry than the first time he'd heard it.

"I'll give you the details tomorrow. Unless you'll let me in right now," he said.

"Good night, Monroe. I think we've said all there is to say for one night, don't you?"

He supposed they had. Besides, Brenda would tell Kim about him any minute now, and that would be that. Cat out of the bag.

"Tomorrow, then."

She closed the door.

Wishing he had another beer to chase away the thrill of being so close to the woman he didn't want to feel anything for, Chaz instead considered calling his brother for a stern reprimand about pleading with any woman for any reason, and for putting himself in such an awkward position.

Big bro Rory, his elder by four years, wouldn't beat around the bush. He'd just reach out and take what he wanted, perfectly willing to suffer the consequences. Then again, Rory at times seemed a little insane.

McKinley had agreed to help out. Soon she'd know that he wasn't only her boss, but the new owner of the agency. His actual title shouldn't make any difference, in theory. Still, she might take the undercover boss business badly.

He could knock again and tell her the truth about this being a test of her willingness to work with him, before Brenda called to tell her the truth of the situation.

What about when he sold the agency, flipping it for a profit, as he'd planned to do? What would happen to her then, if she didn't back down first?

By helping Kim now, he'd be doing a good deed. So how the hell did he turn this situation around? Seriously, was that impossible?

As Chaz headed for the elevator, he had to concede that he'd at least given this a shot. But he didn't make it to the elevator before hearing a door open. He turned to see Kim standing with her hands on her hips in the hallway, her pallor ghostly white, her lips parted for a speech she didn't make.

In that moment, he thought how magnificent she looked, even in anger.

# Six

Fighting off a round of pure, livid anger, Kim faced Chaz Monroe with a distance of thirty feet separating them. Her pulse thudded annoyingly in her neck and wrists.

"You're a bastard," she said. "Is this a game for you? Tell me that much."

"It wasn't a game until you kissed me back and then pulled out that recorder," he replied.

The door to the apartment next to Kim's opened, and her neighbor looked out. Kim smiled wanly at the man. "Having a difference of opinion," she said, explaining the noise.

"A lover's spat," Monroe clarified.

"Please do it elsewhere," the old guy said, retreating back inside. "You're spoiling my dinner."

She pointed a finger at Monroe. "How did you get that tape recording? Did you plant bugs all over the building to keep an eye on things?"

"I did nothing of the sort," he said. "It just happened to fall into my possession."

"Like hell it did."

"Maybe I should come in," he suggested. "We're beyond lawsuits, don't you think? Unless…"

"Unless what?" she snapped.

"Unless you're afraid you'll do what you said on that recording."

"What are you talking about?"

"Seducing me."

"Get over yourself, Monroe. That wasn't a plan, it was girl talk."

"Yet you accomplished it," he pointed out, shaking his way-too-handsome head and dislodging a strand of shaggy hair that fell becomingly across his forehead. It didn't help her cause that he in no way looked like a monster.

Nor did Monroe look as smug as she had expected him to. Frankly, he didn't appear to be pleased with his behavior any more than she was. He didn't grin or let on what he might be thinking, though she did see something in his expression that left her short of breath.          .

"You didn't think—" Her voice faltered. She started over. "You didn't come here to—"

"As a matter of fact, I think I must have," he replied.

"Dream on." Kim placed a hand over her heart in disbelief as her body produced a quake of longing so intense for that very thing they were both thinking, she nearly gasped aloud.

Was it possible to despise a guy and want to bed him at the same time? Monroe had this ultrasexy thing going on that affected her as if it were magical. But he was clouding her judgment and preying on her attraction to him. Obviously, he knew about that weakness. He had heard her conversation with Brenda, where she had wistfully mentioned his looks.

And then again, there had been the kiss.

Kim widened her stance with a crisp show of authority she didn't actually feel. The red dress strained at the seams.

"Letting me in would be a fitting end to this stalemate," Monroe suggested.

Kim glanced down the hallway. Anytime now her nosy neighbor would be back in his doorway. She had to move this conversation out of the open, yet was afraid to get closer to the gorgeous guy who had mesmerized her into facing him again. This meeting went against every principle she had erected to protect herself.

"Letting you in would also be business blasphemy," she said.

"Fortunately, I'm no longer talking about the business, Kim. Neither are you, I'm thinking."

Monroe closed the distance between them with long strides. He was terribly seductive, even when he pleaded his case so crassly. His features and his body were damn near perfect. She hadn't found a single physical flaw in the entire package, except for the shirt, visible beneath his open jacket, which still bore the creases from when she'd grabbed him earlier.

He possessed a damnable, pit-bullish persistence. She wasn't at all sure about the state of his mind.

Or hers.

"Look, Kim," Monroe said, "I can hardly explain how much I want to put business aside for just this one night, call a truce and get to know you better. That's the truth."

Kim's mind sluggishly tripped through rules of negotiation. Should she toss caution to the wind and maul Monroe in the hallway? In the midst of thanking her lucky stars that he hadn't yet reached her, her traitorous body had started to sag. She leaned a shoulder against the doorjamb and considered the ramifications of taking Monroe up on his offer. What could it hurt to speak to him further if she was going to leave the agency, anyway?

It wasn't as if she *cared* for Monroe, beyond her acute physical craving for him. Allowing him inside might be a fitting end to all this infuriating heat and drama.

He stood before her wearing a questioning expression, one eyebrow raised.

"Monroe," she began. "I'm not sure what's going on."

Her neighbor's door opened. Kim tossed him a friendly wave. Sighing heavily in resignation, she wrapped her hands in Monroe's coat and hauled him inside her apartment, hoping she hadn't gone completely insane.

The first thing Chaz noticed was the sweet smell of her apartment. The second was how his body had ended up pressed tightly to Kim's against the wall beside the front door that slammed shut behind them.

They were body to body, without an inch of space between, and below his waist, pertinent body parts were already thankful. Tight against her like that, he couldn't think about business, what her home looked like or about mistrusting her. In fact, he'd just discovered that he was no longer able to trust himself. His body had the lead on this one, and his mind seemed curiously foggy about the future.

Kim's long-lashed hazel eyes, mostly green, remained fixed on him. Her expression was hard to read. Her soft lips finally parted, and sensing another excuse coming that might end the highly sensual, highly addictive position he found himself in, Chaz didn't let her voice a protest. He pressed his index finger to her mouth and shook his head. "Now's not the time," he whispered. "Backward is never the right direction."

She offered him an expression that fell precariously close to being a grimace, and at the same time eyed him warily. But Kim's mind, it seemed to him, had to be in the gutter, next to his.

Wonder Woman was in his grasp, and had welcomed it. Her lips weren't pouty, exactly, but close to it, and relatively ruby-tinted, though he had kissed some of the color away in the bar. Her chest, against his, strained at the confines of the red dress. She breathed shallowly, in shudders.

"What do you propose we do about this?" she asked, biting down on her lower lip hard enough to leave an imprint of teeth marks.

"Are any tape recorders running?" he said.

She glared at him in a way that did nothing to ruin the glorious beauty of her pert oval face. Her ivory neck pulsed with a racing heartbeat. Feeling the firmness of her breasts pressed to his chest, Chaz knew the time for talk was over.

In a smooth motion, he slid one arm around her waist.

The other arm followed. He stroked her slender back with his open palm in a gradual downward glide over the red silk that had been such an inspiration, and now seemed like an unnecessary barrier between them and their crazy, wayward desires.

He found the silk warm and fragrant, the texture exotic. Around them, the room felt cool, dim and distant. Between them, the fires of lustful attraction beat at the air.

Kim shivered as his fingers trailed down her spine. This time when her lips parted, a sigh of resignation emerged. Chaz watched her intently, holding on to his control with every ounce of willpower he possessed.

*Just a little longer...*

All he needed was one more little sign that she actually agreed to what was going to happen next.

He felt downright greedy now that he'd gotten this far. He wanted more of Kim McKinley, and getting closer than this wasn't possible unless it became acceptable for two objects to actually occupy the same space at the same time. He yearned to be inside her, and to enjoy all of her. He hoped they'd settle for nothing less.

She closed her eyes in a flutter of long lashes. Her body swayed as if, parallel to his reactions, she had moved beyond the point of no return. She placed her hands on his hips, but didn't push him away. She gave a slight tug, as though she shared his desire to relish the physicality of the moment.

This was the sign he had been waiting for.

He kissed her.

Not a soft, tender kiss, but a hungry devouring one. There was no hesitancy in McKinley's response. She allowed this mouth-to-mouth exploration and joined in, meeting him in a white-hot dance of lips and tongues and fire, giving as much as receiving.

The McKinley he had wished for in his wildest dreams

kissed him with a fury backed by her own level of greed. As his hands moved over her fine, sleek body, she rubbed up against him, fanning the flames of his raging desires.

Chaz could not recall ever feeling this way. Never this greedy, this needy, or this consumed.

The woman was driving him crazy....

And the damn dress was in the way.

Wanting to feel the smoothness of her skin beneath the slinky fabric, Chaz slowly began to raise the hem upward, over her thighs, toward her hips, listening to the rustle of the expensive silk. He couldn't see the lace he hoped would be underneath, though he located its delicate pattern with his fingers.

*Lace...*

Narrow strips of elastic crossed her hips, holding the dainty lingerie in place. His fingers slipped under, sliding down the cleft that led to her feminine heat from the back.

She groaned. Their mingling breath was volcanic. He breathed hard and fast, ready to explode, and hadn't even seen her naked. Kim was like catnip, with her mouth, her flawless skin and her inferno-like heat.

He desperately wanted all of her, and knew he couldn't take the time. His pulsating body wouldn't allow for the slowness of a proper bedding. Plus, no bedroom was in sight.

He shifted his hands to find the zipper at her back. The zipper made no sound as he eased it downward.

Dragging his mouth from hers, he took seconds to study her face, wondering if Kim was truly going to allow this, not quite believing his luck. He felt compelled to speak. "It will be worth it," he said. "All the best things are."

Her wide-eyed gaze unflinchingly met his. "Then why are you dallying?" Her voice was low-pitched and sensuously breathy.

"Is that what I'm doing?" he asked.

"Don't you know?"

"I'm afraid you'll change your mind. Should I give you that option?"

"Why, when you're so barbaric about everything else?"

Chaz's physical urges escalated with the flirty tone of their repartee. It was to be a fight to the very end between them if their minds got in the way.

One of his hands remained on the zipper. He tilted her head back with his other one, with his fingers under her chin. "Maybe we can pretend we're just two people enjoying each other."

"Maybe I should have chugged that martini."

"Was that your first?"

"Kiss?"

"Martini."

"It couldn't actually be the first if I didn't drink it."

Chaz tilted her head back farther, wanting to see deep into Kim's soul through the pools of green in her eyes.

"And the kiss?" he said.

"Are you now asking for an accounting of other things in my personal life?"

"I'm jealous just thinking about your personal life."

He eased the zipper the rest of the way down. Kim's hands, on his hips, hadn't moved again. Each turn of her head sent her lush scent scattering. Chaz inhaled her woodsy fragrance and felt it mix with the rising heat waves inside his chest. Talk couldn't really spoil this for him. Nothing could. The deepness of her voice was a vibration that made him want her more than ever.

He feathered his lips over her forehead and placed a series of kisses on her cheek in a trail that led back to her mouth—not entirely sure why she allowed this kind of liberty.

She had a small waist and delicate bones. Touching her gave him a thrill equal to being caught in a lightning storm.

This wasn't love, it was lust, he reminded himself. Love didn't leave a man breathless and overheated. He'd always figured love as a lukewarm emotional state that developed slowly over time between long-standing acquaintances. He and Kim didn't know each other. They had barely spoken a few hundred words, total, and were acting on instinct.

"This is a truce," he said, brushing her mouth with his. "A white flag."

In a replay of the kiss in the bar, he rested his lips on hers lightly before drawing back far enough to note her response. Her eyes were half-closed now. Her lashes were blackened by eye makeup she didn't need to enhance her appearance. Her skin gleamed as though their steamy encounter had moistened it. Up close, she really did look younger. She looked…delicious.

The red dress, he decided in a whirlwind of thought, probably wouldn't hold a candle to Kim in a baggy T-shirt and nothing else. Kim with her hair mussed, getting out of bed on a weekend morning, or emerging from a shower, wet and soapy.

Those thoughts turned him on.

He wedged his thigh between her legs and pressed her roughly to the wall. Her mouth molded to his, and her mouth was a marvel. She nipped at his lips, breathing sultry streams of air into him.

Her hands found their way underneath his coat, and tugged at his shirt. Finding bare skin, her fingers splayed, hot as pokers, and sent streaks of pleasure soaring through him.

Who needed control when faced with *this?*

What man wouldn't consider giving up a future for a night like this one?

Liking how light she felt in his arms, he lifted her up. Her legs encircled his thighs. The spot he achingly wanted to reach settled over his erection as he held her close, though there were still too many clothes in the way.

Backing up a step made things worse. Part of him wanted to hold her like this forever, culmination be damned. But he was also aware of how close they had come to losing the chance of working anything out after this ferocious sexual escapade.

His mind's chatter stopped abruptly when her mouth separated from his and moved to his ear. Her lips flitted over his lobe teasingly before she came back for more, her mouth hungrier this time, their kiss resembling the furor of anger in its intensity.

She was giving in, meeting him halfway as an aggressor. He had never desired anything so badly as to be inside her. Surely there was a place to finish this—a sofa or a rug?

He caressed her, devoured her, his elation escalating. Her fingers dipped under his waistband, searching, scorching, ensuring his hardness, driving him mad. The only sound in the room was the rasp of their breathing. The only sensation left to him was Kim McKinley in his arms.

And then the air shook with the shrill sound of a phone ringing. The sound echoed loudly throughout the room.

Chaz's heart missed a beat. His lips stalled. It was Kim's phone, and a bad omen, he just knew.

The click of an answering machine turning on followed the second ring.

"Kim?" a voice said, loud enough for Brenda Chang to have been in the room with them.

"Kim, are you there? Pick up the damn phone! Listen. Monroe isn't who we think he is. He isn't the VP. He's the new owner of the agency, and is occupying that office in order to spy on the masses. He owns the agency and us, lock, stock and barrel. Kim, please pick up! Monroe might be on his way over there. I wanted to catch you before he arrives and pass on that news. Kim? Oh, hell. Tell Sam. Don't answer the door. Where are you? Call me back."

By the time the machine turned off, Kim's tight hold on him had gone slack. She stiffened so fast, her actions didn't register until her legs loosened, and he had to press her against the wall to support her.

Some of her glorious heat slipped from his grasp. Her eyes were averted, her lids lowered. Once she had regained her feet, she got her hands up between them.

She couldn't seem to catch a breath. Her chest still strained against his. When she finally looked up, her big eyes met his as if searching for something. Her pallor brought a whole new meaning to the word pale, despite the splashes of pink in her cheeks.

"Kim," he said, addressing her accusatory gaze. "It's okay. I knew Brenda was going to tell you. My role at the agency is supposed to be a secret for now. I wanted to get to know the workings of the place and play catch up."

"You own the agency?" The words tumbled out between harsh breaths.

"Yes."

"You're not the vice president?"

"No."

Her eyes projected an expression of betrayal. She blinked slowly. When she spoke, her voice shook. "Get out. I think you'd better get out right now."

"Kim—"

"You can see the door. Use it," she directed. "Please."

He held up both hands in a placating gesture, and tried to find the right words to ease the tension. No words came. Kim didn't look angry about this, she looked ill.

"Now," she repeated.

He had to explain, had to make her see. "I bought the company to make it better, more successful. The position you want is still on the table. I'll make a decision once I get a grip on the rest of the agency's personnel needs and can move things forward. We already have a truce, you and I, so we're in the clear about the situation. Nothing has changed."

"Oh, we're far from clear about anything," she countered. "And everything has changed."

"That doesn't have to be the case."

"Doesn't it? You were going to sleep with me, withholding a secret like that. You let me think you took my job, and you were willing to let me hang myself and my profession by directing me toward a bed."

"A date with a bed has nothing to do with work or the issues there," he protested.

She sucked in a big breath of air and lowered her voice. "What was this all about then, for you? A test of my character? You wanted to see if I'd actually sleep my way up the ladder? Maybe you wondered if I'd done it before, and that's why I had been promised your office?"

Chaz stared at her, sensing she wasn't finished.

"Are you so naïve that you'd actually believe I could remain at the agency after sleeping with you? That being here with you, like this, wouldn't affect my reputation, or reach the ears of the other employees, and eventually my clients? Or that it would all go away if you were to promote me now?"

"Kim, listen—"

She shook her head. "Tell me this, Monroe—is there actually a holiday party to cater?"

"There could be," he said, hating the way that sounded.

She turned her face. "Please leave."

Chaz's stomach tightened with pangs of regret over the way he had approached this, understanding how it must look to Kim. In his defense, he'd been smitten, for lack of a better word to describe the immediacy of his attraction to her. Had certain parts of his anatomy made him come here, under the premise of testing her work ethic? Could he have slipped that far?

She had told him to get out. What other option did he have after a command like that, except to do as she asked? His explanation hadn't swayed her. She was angry. Her eyes blazed. Kim was hurt, half-naked and feeling the need to protect herself from further harm…and he'd been less than stellar in his approach to this whole situation.

It was obvious she took into consideration things he hadn't thought over before showing up here and placing his hands on her. Also clear now, after what she'd said, was the idea that she might have opened herself to him because she truly hadn't planned on returning to her job. In that case, a liaison to explore the sparks between them would have been okay for her.

That had been ruined by one simple withheld truth.

*Damn it.*

"I'm attracted to you." Chaz retreated a step. "I'll confess that here and mean it. I wanted to get to know you, and still do. But what you're thinking wasn't what brought me here. I wasn't going to use you for some sordid purpose."

Her eyes met his. "Here's the thing, Monroe. Some women probably do sleep their way to the top, and I'm telling you now that I'm not one of them. In fact, it looks as though I've just kissed my way to the bottom."

His hands remained suspended in the air. Chaz had prided himself on being decent at handling people, yet had botched the hell out of this situation. He supposed that's what came of mixing lust with work.

He had known better and ignored the signs, but he wasn't an idiot or completely ruled by what was in his pants. He did comprehend her take on this predicament, and it was a damn shame, because in her mind the damage had been done, and he wasn't going to allow himself to beg her to change her mind.

A man could only go so far.

"Okay," he conceded, reaching for the doorknob. "Though you might not believe this, I am sorry the news has upset you. My purpose was never to hurt or demean you. And from everything I've heard about your job performance, you've proven your talent and superior work ethic to justify being in line for the promotion."

He really did not want to leave, especially like this. He gave her one last lingering look before opening the door, hoping she might soften. "No one needs to know about this. I'm not a kiss-and-tell kind of guy, and you can trust me on that. I've apologized. I've confessed to liking you. I guess what you do with that is up to you."

With a frown of disappointment etched on his brow, Chaz closed the door on what might have turned out to be the hottest night in history.

In the hallway, he slapped the wall and uttered a choice four-letter oath. This night had not gone well. In fact, it couldn't have been worse.

McKinley wanted him. Of that there was no doubt. She had been willing to take him in and take him on. Perhaps, now that she knew the score, she would come around. They could pretend this never happened and start over.

*Or maybe not.*

Seeing her at work might bring on his feelings of lust for her all over again. He wouldn't be able to touch her, talk to her privately or smell her rich fragrance up close, if she returned to the job.

Things were truly messed up, yet he couldn't go back and demand to be let back in. It was too late for that.

Sighing in frustration, he walked to the waiting elevator and stepped inside. Kim didn't open her door and call after him this time. It was like a slap in the face—the second in two hours. He didn't have to take that lying down. He shouldn't have to. He would move on and forget her.

Staring blankly at her door, Chaz rolled his shoulders. Something was definitely wrong with him. Despite arguments to the contrary, he'd already started imagining a strategy for getting Kim back, if not at the office, where she ultimately belonged, then into that baggy T-shirt he'd envisioned—and the naughty red shoes.

At the very least, he had to know what this was about, what her dislike of the holiday work meant. Research would be the key to unlocking Kim McKinley's secrets, and he had plenty of know-how at his fingertips.

"Nobody hates Christmas," he muttered as the elevator descended. "Not even you, Kim. I'll just have to prove that to you."

Kim slid down the wall, staring at the door the devil had just used to make his exit. Chaz Monroe was a monster, and she had been foolish to believe anything else.

He had almost succeeded in making her forget the hovering darkness of the season, and about men being liars when given the chance. She had been willing to share tonight with him under the waving flag of truce and the lure of the laws of man-woman attraction. And look where that had landed her.

Monroe had spoiled things, in essence tromping over her mother's grave in motorcycle boots and kicking up clods of freshly turned earth. She could hear her mother shouting *I told you so.*

Head in her hands, knees drawn to her chest, Kim sat without moving for a long time before finding the strength to get up. She had wanted so badly to believe that her mother didn't have to be right.

She walked to the kitchen and removed aluminum foil from the top of a pan on the counter. Turning slowly, she hit a lever with her bare foot and dumped the entire batch of frosted Christmas cookies into the trash.

"Lesson learned the hard way," she said, slipping out of the red dress and leaving the puddle of silk discarded on the hardwood floor.

# Seven

She was supposed to be on vacation starting at noon the next day, and debated whether to show up at the office at all. After spending a sleepless night thinking about it, she had decided to go in.

If she was lucky, she'd beat Monroe to the office and be able to pick up a few things. She also needed to put the finishing touch on a project before heading out to take the vacation time due to her. At least she'd get something in terms of a paycheck before finding out if she'd have to terminate her employment.

But she was angry enough at the moment to keep the job and drive Monroe crazy, just to spite him.

Entering the building quickly, Kim hustled into the first open elevator. She got off on her floor and sighed with relief to find the hallway empty that led to the little cubicle that had been her home away from home for the last few years.

Monroe had said the next step was hers, so she'd ignore him and get on with things more or less as usual, for as long as she could. Time away would be necessary, and would allow her to set up a barrier between herself and the agency's new owner until they both cooled off. If more bad news was to come her way, it would have to find her someplace else.

In order to get unemployment money, she needed to be fired.

At the entrance to her cubicle, she stopped short. Brenda sat in her chair with her arms and legs crossed.

"You did not, in fact, call me back," Brenda said. "I worried all night."

Kim leaned a hip against what couldn't really be called

a doorjamb. It seemed there was no escaping some of what she'd hoped to avoid.

"Did you get my message?" Brenda asked.

"I got it."

"Did he show up?"

Kim nodded.

"Did you let him in?"

Kim nodded.

"Is that why you don't look so good?" Brenda asked frankly.

"Trust me, I feel even worse."

"So, you aren't going to speak to me ever again?"

The question got Kim's attention. So did the tone. "Is there a reason I shouldn't?"

"No. Well, maybe. But he swore all he wanted to do was keep you here, like I do, so I was with him on that one."

Brenda had done something bad and felt regretful—and that was the reason for her early arrival—though Brenda wouldn't have done anything to hurt her on purpose.

Kim's thoughts returned to the dress, the shoes…and then to the tape recorder Monroe had in his possession last night and her idea that he might have bugged her office in order to have captured conversations on tape.

"He got the tape from you, Bren," she said.

"Oh, crap." Brenda covered her face with her hands. "Yes, he did."

"Because?"

"I believed him. He seemed sincere when he said he wants to keep you here. I know he likes you. The way he looked at you in the bar was…"

"Inappropriate?"

"No. I don't think so," Brenda said. "Not exactly. More like he was awed."

Kim's heart shuddered with the memory of how blind-sided by Monroe's sexual magnetism she had been as she stood against that wall in her apartment with Monroe's hands and mouth all over her. After anger, embarrassment sat high on her list of emotions to avoid at night when attempting to count sheep.

She nailed Brenda with her gaze. "Cough it up, Bren. What else don't I know?"

"In his email yesterday he asked if I'd attend the meeting in the bar, then let you two work things out if the meeting went well. That's why I left. Well, that and I was trying to avoid watching you two going for the other person's jugular. Honestly, though, I wasn't sure you noticed I had gone."

"Moot point. It didn't work out, anyway," Kim said. "Monroe's a barbarian when it comes to negotiation."

*And also a sexual barbarian,* Kim inwardly added. The moniker probably fit, due to all those Celtic genes behind a name like *Monroe* that conjured images of men with blue faces. Marauding Vikings. People with wooden clubs.

Brenda looked up. "You're not going to do that party?"

"There was no party, Bren. I think that was a sham to see if I'd bend over backward."

Brenda's eyes went wide with surprise. She echoed Kim's word for Monroe. "Barbarian!"

"I suppose you didn't know for sure if there actually was a spur-of-the-moment holiday project?" Kim pressed.

Brenda crossed her heart with her index finger. "I most certainly don't know anything about that. I'm so sorry for having anything to do with last night. Really sorry."

Kim sighed. "It's okay. I almost fell for his line, too."

That was the hard part, the unacceptable part of this mess. She had sort of fallen for Monroe, despite his antics. She liked the angles of his handsome, slightly rugged face, and the shaggy hair surrounding it that often fell across his forehead. She liked the way his wide shoulders stretched his shirt, and the warmth of his hands on the exposed skin of her lower back.

She liked his voice and the easy way it affected her.

Heck, she might have fallen far enough to have assumed she'd be working on a project dealing with the North Pole today. If Brenda hadn't left that warning message in time, she might have ended up naked on the floor next to the new owner of this place, with nothing to show for it but a bruised backside.

*The thought of that...*

"What happened after you let him in?" Brenda's voice seemed distant, drowned out by the sound of Kim's heartbeat, which suddenly seemed uncharacteristically loud. It had been a mistake to think about Monroe.

"I got your message, Bren," she said, "and he left."

Brenda looked relieved. "You're still here, then? You didn't quit?"

"Not for the next several days. I'm going to take my vacation."

"This would be the first time you did."

"It's time."

Her heartbeat refused to settle down. Why?

She inhaled a breath of—not Christmas In A Can, but something else. A masculine scent. One she recognized.

*Oh.*

She saw her fear confirmed in the look on Brenda's face.

"There's someone behind me, isn't there?" Kim said.

"Yep."

Turning slowly, Kim's gaze met with the top button of Chaz Monroe's perfectly pressed blue- and white-striped shirt.

"Miss McKinley," Chaz said, reverting to formality to get over the shock of seeing her in the building after last night's anticlimactic rebuff.

Here she was, and he felt slightly taken aback.

"Mr. Monroe," she said, refusing to glance up at him as she took a step back.

She was perfectly tidy, dressed in a knee-length black skirt and a lavender sweater that covered her hips and other notable curves. Her fair hair fell softly toward her shoulders in a sheet of gold. The lips that had mesmerized him were freshly stained pink.

She looked ravishing. No evidence of a sleepless night showed on her face. There were no dark circles under her eyes. Not one eyelash seemed out of place. Had she dismissed him and what had nearly transpired between them so quickly, when he hadn't slept a wink? When his thoughts never strayed from her, and what he might say if she showed her pretty face on this floor?

Chaz cleared his throat. "You're working today?"

She still hadn't glanced up, though Chaz sensed she wanted to meet his eyes as much as he wanted her to. The electricity crackling between them hadn't diminished because of what had happened the night before. If anything, it was worse.

His wish list hadn't changed, he realized. His lust for this woman was now the size of a bloated balloon. Office or no office, and decorum be damned, he desired Kim McKinley more than ever. He'd start to work on that mouth of hers if given the opportunity, and torture it into a grin. He would offer half his earnings to be able to earn her smile, her trust, and to hear her laugh.

"I'm only in for an hour, then I'm off on that vacation I mentioned," she said, her voice unreasonably calm.

"Are you going someplace nice?"

"I'm going home," she said.

Brenda got to her feet, as if that were her cue to jump in. "I'll help with those last-minute details, Kim, so that you can get out of here."

They were presenting a united front against him. For

a minute, he actually envied Brenda her closeness to the woman he had come near to bedding. Again, though, it was a new day, and he'd deal.

"Okay. Have a good time." His tone was commendably casual, reflecting professional interest and nothing more. "By the way, have you decided on whether you'll be returning after that vacation?"

"I'm thinking on it. I'll be sure to let you know."

Kim's tone suggested to him that she wasn't going to let him ruin a good thing if she could help it, and also that she expected him to mind his manners if she did decide to keep her job.

*Checkmate.*

"Great. I'm sorry the party didn't work out for you," he said. "Maybe next time."

Kim raised her chin defiantly. Their gazes connected. Chaz rode out the next jolt that came with the blaze of inquiry he saw in those greenish eyes. He didn't want to push her buttons. Not now. Research awaited him. He had been able to access a few things about her background in those sleepless hours of the night, though nothing personal enough to give him a leg up on her issues.

"Yes. Maybe next time," she said.

He inclined his head and muttered in parting, "Ladies."

When he turned, he felt Kim's eyes on him in a gaze intense enough to burn a hole in his back. She was angrier than ever, though she looked to be in control of her emotions this morning. They were continuing to play this strange game with each other, with the outcome unclear.

This wasn't over. Not by a long shot. If she returned after that vacation, he would probably desire her more. When she left, he'd miss the spark of whatever existed between them.

Did this make him a lust-sick idiot?

He shrugged.

Back in his office, Chaz picked up the phone and hit a

number on speed dial. He hated to make this call, since he'd been trying to beat big brother Rory at his own game for more than a year…and maybe all his life. Other than his own personal need to be successful, Rory was always in the background setting the gold standard as far as the family business was concerned. Those business dealings weren't actually supposed to achieve the status of a competitive sport, but things between the brothers had turned out that way.

However, this wasn't *all* about business.

A male voice on the line answered in a brisk tone. "It's early, bro."

"I need some help, Rory. As my elder, I'm sure you're obliged to listen, in spite of the hour."

"I've been at work for three hours already, Chaz. It's not like I just got up. I call this early-rising routine CEO Stamina. It does my heart good to see that you're getting with the program."

Chaz sat back in his chair. "I need some intel."

"On a company?"

"On a woman."

Rory chuckled without bothering to hide it. "Well, that's a first. But you do know how to use the internet?"

"Tried that, and nothing pertinent turned up. I'd like to use your information source."

"Must be an interesting woman," Rory remarked.

"She's an employee."

"Do you suspect agency espionage?"

"I suspect she might have an interesting background that forces the issue of a contractual dispute."

"Is this employee attractive?" Rory asked.

"Would that matter to your source?"

"Nope. Does it matter to you?" Rory countered.

"Nope. So do I have your permission to contact Sarah?"

"With my blessing. And bro?"

"Yeah?"

"What's your ETA for getting that agency ready to flip? I have another business you might be interested in when you get the money out of your first big acquisition."

Hell, he had only owned this agency for a week.

"Still working on it," he said. "It's too early to tell how long it might take."

"Well, it doesn't pay to hang on for too long. You might become vested and actually see yourself as the head of a firm. Buy, fix and sell is the key."

"The family mantra," Chaz agreed, unwilling to think about the ramifications of Kim finding out he had planned all along to sell the company once it was on its feet.

"Want some more unasked-for advice?" Rory said.

"I'm all ears."

"Mom would appreciate a call now and then. She says it's been two weeks."

"Wherever does time go?" Chaz muttered before disconnecting.

That hadn't gone too badly.

As for Kim, he didn't really owe her anything. He just wanted to play fair. In pursuit of fairness, he'd get the intel on her lined up. Sarah Summers was Rory's secret weapon for finding things out. A grad student at M.I.T., Sarah specialized in what amounted to cloak-and-dagger information trading. She might be considered a hacker for her rogue-like pursuits, but no one was quite sure how she did what she did, and the results were more than satisfying. Over the last couple years, her reports had added a lot of bucks to the Monroe family business coffers.

If Kim had anything in her background to find, Sarah would be the one to find it. Chaz didn't need any more office intrigue or rumors spreading about that casting couch Kim mentioned. The situation would be out of his hands until Sarah got back to him. In the meantime, Kim would be gone, and he'd be able to keep his mind where it belonged…on business. Definitely not on McKinley's ultra-hot body, or the look in her eyes when Brenda's call had come in last night—the look showcasing betrayal and pain.

Other than Kim and Brenda, not one person at the agency knew he had bought this company in order to turn a quick profit, and that he hadn't planned on remaining here for long. He sure as hell didn't plan on becoming too comfortable, or being overly involved with employees' personalities. He had just inadvertently gotten stuck on the issue of a very tempting blonde.

After the sale, and after he departed, Kim might gain access to the job she coveted. Win-win? He'd move on, and she'd move up. If she got her promotion with somebody else in charge, he'd be off the hook, and this would work in his favor in terms of the possibility of getting to know her better.

That scenario might, in fact, solve everything.

But, his annoying inner chatter reminded him, Kim would probably still have to capitulate on the holiday clause in her contract, or risk being overlooked for the promotion by the next owner. She'd be hurt all over again. She'd be crushed.

Interestingly enough, he couldn't stand the thought of Kim suffering.

He had gone soft.

It looked a lot like Chaz Monroe cared too much about his employees already. Some of them, anyway.

*One of them.*

Chaz rubbed his temple as he stared at the phone. Certainly it appeared as though big brother Rory didn't linger for long on those kinds of things. If he did, he never spoke about it, or let on. Then again, it was entirely possible that Rory wasn't human. Did Chaz actually want to emulate the successful business profile of an alien?

He absently tapped on the desk with his fingers. He had not lied to anyone here. Owners went undercover all the time to ferret out business details. With the agency running smoothly and well in the black, the next owner would be crazy not to keep things the way they were.

As for Kim, the best thing for her and his conscience both would be to help her in any way he could, and then back away. He'd have to shelve his feelings for her in order to make sure she got what she deserved. And okay, so he was way too addicted to her. He could hide that, get over that.

At least he could try.

Leaning forward, he punched another number into the phone and waited until someone picked up. "Mom," he said, "about that party…"

# Eight

"She's gone," Brenda said when Chaz appeared in her cubicle an hour later. It was probably just as well, he decided, because he hadn't actually thought out what he'd say to her now that he was here.

In spite of the arguments and his sense of fairness where Kim was concerned, he wasn't ready to just let her go away, maybe for good, without dealing with her future at the agency. Until he heard back from his intel source, he was willing to try to change her mind on this holiday issue one more time. The Monroes never backed away from a good fight, especially if there was a reward at the end.

"Fine," he said to Brenda, reordering his thoughts on the new challenge and how he'd have to play it. "It's you I came to see, anyway. Can you help me in Kim's place with the party event?"

Brenda raised an eyebrow. "The party that is no party?"

"Oh, there's a party, all right. Did she tell you there wasn't?"

Brenda swiveled in her chair. "Now I'm confused. But just so you know, I won't do anything else that involves my best friend's feelings for you or her job."

Chaz withheld a grin. "She has feelings for me?"

"You don't want to know about the name-calling," Brenda replied. "From both of us."

"I suppose I deserved that for my behavior at her apartment, but there is a party, and I do need help. Can I count on you?"

Brenda blinked slowly. "Depends. Are you offering the same deal you gave Kim? Time off after the holidays and a nice bonus?"

"Yes. Okay. Same deal."

"You'll sign that in blood? Your blood?"

"Brenda, I might remind you that I'm the owner of this place and have something better than blood."

"Power?"

He smiled.

"And we're not supposed to know about you owning the agency, or let that get around, right?" Brenda said sheepishly. "Though a couple of us do know that?"

"You're a heartbreaker, Chang. I had no idea blackmail made the world go around."

"I believe I said *nice* bonus."

"To which I agreed."

"So, will you appear at my apartment if I refuse, and…?"

"Never. That's a promise."

"Darn." Brenda smiled back. "Oh well, with an offer like that, how can I refuse? I may have to use the bonus to help support my friend if she leaves the job."

"I'm not sure Kim would like our deal," he said.

"I'm positive she won't," Brenda agreed. And the really good part, Chaz knew, was that Brenda wouldn't be able to resist running to Kim with this bit of news. He only hoped that Kim might react the way he hoped she would, and face him down. Again. At least he'd get more time with her if that happened.

Fighting with her was better than not seeing her at all, he had just that minute decided. *At least in theory.*

Kim hustled to the floor beneath her office, where the art department had their space. Just one more detail to take care of, and Monroe would be out of her hair for at least seven days. She wouldn't have to think about him, dream about him or convince herself to despise him.

Going home to her mother's meant dealing with things she had been avoiding since her mother's death. She hadn't set foot in that house since, and had dreaded going there for ages before that.

Because Kim was an only child, the house and all of her mother's belongings were now hers. She should have relished combing through her mother's things for remembered treasures. The fact that she didn't look forward to it piled on more guilt.

She read somewhere that emotions can attach to objects, and she wanted nothing that might remind her of the problems they had shared. Had she loved her mother? Absolutely, and maybe too much. Witnessing the level of her mom's nearly constant self-inflicted pain and suffering had become too much for one daughter to bear. She hadn't been able to keep up with the treatments and the arguments and the ups and downs of her mother's diagnosis of clinical depression.

This was the season that had kicked off the whole thing in the first place. December. Christmas. Betrayal. Would those things be contagious with her mother gone? Did houses retain the sorrow and joys of the people who had lived in them, or would her mother's house be just a house, empty and waiting to be dealt with?

She had given that house six months to let loose of its old memories and feelings. It was high time she dealt with this.

The art department had been waiting for her, and took less time than she had anticipated to finish up what she needed. On her way out, someone stopped her with a painting on a piece of white cardboard and a question.

"Do you like this rendering?" Mark Ogilvie asked, showing her the board. "It was done super quickly, but I thought I'd run it by you before you left on vacation."

"Sorry, Mark?" Kim took the board.

"The special Christmas party you and Brenda are doing as a favor to Monroe."

"I'm not sure what you're talking about." Kim flipped

the board upright. It took her a minute to understand what she was seeing. Then it dawned. On that board was a watercolor rendering of the party Monroe had asked her to do. The party that she believed wasn't really a party, and a complete sham.

Decorated tables, wrapped packages, ice sculptures, servers dressed up like elves—all of this had been painted in sparkling detail from Mark's artistic point of view, and it was a beautiful, magical wonderland.

Her heart stuttered. She sucked in a breath. Closing her eyes briefly, Kim handed the painting back to Mark. "This has nothing to do with me. Sorry."

He looked perplexed. "Can you get it to Brenda then, if you're on your way back up? She requested it about twenty minutes ago as a top priority."

"I don't think Brenda…" Kim didn't finish the protest. "Twenty minutes ago, you said?"

"She told me to show it to you on your way out. She made me promise to catch you before you reached the elevator."

Kim forced a smile. "Okay. Thanks. This looks terrific, Mark. I'll take it right up to her. I'm sure Brenda will tell you the same thing."

It took every ounce of strength she possessed to walk toward the elevator with the painting in hand. Brenda had given her a heads-up on some new turn in the tide, and this painting said it all. Monroe was at it again, with Brenda this time.

Had Brenda somehow fallen for his line? After not getting his way with her, had Monroe moved on to her friend with hopes of luring Brenda into bed?

"Monster!"

When the elevator arrived, Kim got on, punched the floor button with the edge of the painting and clenched her teeth. Monroe's antics were so unacceptable they were the definition of ludicrous. She wasn't going to take this lying down. Neither would Brenda.

She wasn't going back to Cubicle City. She'd ram this painting down Chaz Monroe's throat for causing yet another hitch in her exit strategy.

"Monster," she repeated, causing two other employees occupying the elevator with her to glance her way. "Brute."

Surely Brenda wouldn't fall for his nonsense after their conversation on the matter of Monroe's lack of integrity and business ethics. Brenda wouldn't have provided this heads-up if Brenda hadn't known the score.

She stormed out of the elevator, strode briskly to the offices and past Monroe's secretary, Alice.

"Kim?" Alice said, standing up.

"Personal matter," Kim tossed back as she reached for the door handle of the office that should have been hers, but now kept the king of jerks tucked inside.

Monroe was there. He stood with his back to the window, watching her as she entered. He was looking more attractive than she had allowed herself to remember from only an hour ago.

Propelled by the thrashing heartbeat in her chest and an uncontrollable wish to see Monroe squirm, Kim crossed to the desk and tossed the painting on top of it.

"What do you think you're doing?" she demanded, sounding winded. "One partial conquest isn't enough for you? You'd suck my best friend into your web, too? What I want to know is if you're doing this to get back at me, or if you're some kind of fiend? Sex fiend, maybe? I'd truly like to understand your actions. I'd like to know how far your lies usually get you."

She saw her mistake as soon as she'd said those words. Monroe wasn't alone. A woman sat in the leather chair beside the desk.

A chill ran down the back of her neck as Kim looked at

the woman, who without standing up said, "You must be Kim McKinley. I'm Dana Monroe. Chaz's mother."

"I..." Words failed Kim. "Excuse me."

She was really damn glad that the door was still open when she turned to rush through.

Chaz steeled his determination not to go after Kim, though he very badly wanted to. The blonde whirlwind had made his heart double up on beats.

"Feisty," his mother said, eyeing him instead of the doorway Kim had fled through. "Witnessing that little tantrum was part of the reason you asked me to rush over here, I suppose?"

"No. Not exactly. But thanks for coming, Mom. Lucky for me you were headed across the street when I called."

"Sex fiend, Chaz?"

"It's a long story."

"You've known her for how long, and she already knows your secrets?"

Chaz grinned. "Those kinds of things might be Rory's secrets, but not mine."

She waved a hand. "That's the woman you'd like to keep?"

"She is good enough at what she does to occupy this office someday."

"Yes, well, I hope she doesn't talk to everyone like that, or I fear there won't be any clients left."

He shrugged. "She's mad at me for being here, in this office, on this floor."

"That's all she's angry about?"

"Possibly not. Again, long story. So, the party is still on?"

"Everyone loves a good party, Chaz, including me. Hand me that picture, and I'll make some calls. I won't be stepping on anyone's toes by putting this together myself?"

"No toes."

"This is all for her? For McKinley?"

Chaz lowered his voice. "I have a feeling it might be the first Christmas party she has ever attended. If I can get her there, that is. She has a sad spot that surfaces when the holiday is mentioned."

"This is a goodwill effort on your part, then?"

"You could say that, yes."

"All right." His mother stood up and waited for Chaz to give her a peck on the cheek. "My sons know I'd do anything for them, and if it's a goodwill mission, so much the better."

On her way out, she paused to get in a longer last word. "You should probably spend less time with Rory. Whatever he has might be starting to rub off on you."

Dressed as well as any woman of substance in New York, diamond earrings, fur-trimmed suit and all, his mother said her farewells and left. Alice filled the doorway soon afterward.

"I suppose you were eavesdropping?" Chaz said.

Alice made a zipping motion across her lips and tossed away an invisible key.

"I suppose you'll be expecting a nice bonus, too, to keep that zipper zipped?" Chaz asked.

Despite the drama of the mouth-closing routine, Alice was able to speak. "Not necessary, since I'm only doing my job."

"Well, that's a relief," Chaz muttered as the door closed, sealing him off from some of the most enigmatic women to ever cross an office threshold.

As a matter of fact, he was starting to feel a little funny about that.

*Now,* he thought, turning back to his desk, if Sarah would call with that intel report on Kim, he might actually have a leg to stand on.

Big reminder here: he had only been in this office for a few days, and his mind had been hijacked for the last two by a woman he wanted to help as much as he wanted to…

Well, until Sarah called, maybe he could get some official work done, and be of use.

Glancing out the window, he smiled. "Hopefully, it will be a merry Christmas, Kim," he whispered as the phone beside him rang and Sarah Summers's number lit up the screen.

Brenda was waiting for Kim in the elevator and pulled the red Stop button once she had entered.

"I've been riding these things up and down for the last twenty minutes, changing elevators every five," Brenda said.

"Thanks for the warning," Kim managed to say before resting her head against the gray metallic wall. "Shall I warn you about him in more detail, Bren?"

"You're kidding, right?"

"Actually, no."

"You imagine I was born yesterday, or that I can't read between the lines? I'm hurt that you'd think I could be a traitor to our friendship, which means more to me than this job."

Kim smiled weakly, thinking about the tape recorder Brenda had given to Monroe.

"So, you're going home?" Brenda asked. "To your mother's house? Would you like me to come with you?"

"Thanks, but no thanks. You said yourself that it's time I face my demons."

"It's the season for joy, Kim," Brenda said. "You could wait until next month to confront those buggers."

"I don't think I have an option. It's now or never, or this might never be behind me. I can see that now."

They were silent as the remark soaked in.

"I won't help him," Brenda said. "I had Mark do the work, and promised that he would get the bonus."

Kim nodded.

"They're not all scoundrels, no matter what you tend to believe," Brenda continued. "The fact that Monroe is attracted to you doesn't mean he's a creep or that he can help it."

"You're taking his side?"

"I'm presenting both sides of what's going on without addressing what's at the core of all this."

"Which is me facing or not facing this damn holiday."

"Yes, and it's good that you know it."

Brenda was right. She had gone along with this fear of Christmas for the past few years, always rallying for Kim and helping to protect her—until now, when the time for frankness and real concern had finally arrived.

"Possibly going home will help," Kim said.

"If you need me, call."

Kim pressed the button. Instead of the elevator moving, the door opened. Chaz Monroe stood there, a serious expression on his devastatingly fine, chiseled face.

# Nine

"Jeez. You'd think there were only three of us in the entire building," Brenda quipped, looking back and forth from Kim to Monroe.

"Will you please excuse us for a minute, Brenda?" Monroe said.

Kim stood very still, afraid to say more of what was on her mind after doing so in his office, in front of one of his family members. In all honesty, she didn't feel angry anymore, anyway; she felt drained. Dealing with Monroe had already taken its toll, and it seemed that toll kept on climbing.

"Kim?" Brenda awaited word on what to do.

"It's okay, Bren. I've got this."

Without further protest, Brenda left the elevator.

The door closed.

Monroe faced her from a distance of two feet; close enough for her to reach out and touch if she dared to confront the feelings she had tamped down in an effort to retain her dignity and sense of self. If she lost that sense of self, she feared what might happen. Would the past bring up trouble or be left behind in favor of something worse?

"I'm sorry," Monroe said, out of the blue.

The apology surprised her. She hadn't expected him to be so frank and straightforward, and had to distrust him, still.

More questions surfaced, like bubbles rising to the top of water, all of them concerning the man across from her.

If she were to start over, to leave the darkness in the distance, would she be setting herself up for a fall?

If she confessed to liking Monroe more than she should

after knowing him for a mere two days—the same man that had teased her, kept things from her and then made her overheat with pleasure on more than one occasion—he might act upon that weakness and take further advantage.

If he realized how difficult it was for her to keep her hands off him, he might throw her against the wall and kiss everything from her lips to her berry-colored toes. Too much kissing, fondling and overheating sexually would mean that their relationship, however temporary, might fizzle equally as fast as it began. Flames this hot tended to burn out quickly. If that happened, her secret dread of ending up like her mother, holed up in a house and simmering in defeat, year after year, alone, would reappear as a possibility.

Tendencies for depression and mental instability sometimes ran in families, she had read. Though she had successfully avoided the symptoms, fear of them had more or less made her an emotional hermit.

The good thing—if there was a good thing to be found here—was that she knew how flawed she was.

"Sorry?" she echoed, wondering if Monroe was sorry for the pressure he was putting on her over her contract or the seductive heat he caused.

Did he regret last night?

"I know I have a problem," she admitted, though the confession was difficult. "I've been trying to work it out, but it hurts me to do so. You'll have to take my word that this isn't some game I'm playing, and that I've protested the change in my contract in earnest."

"Can we forget the blasted contract for a minute?" he said.

Kim glanced up at him from beneath her lashes.

"I'm not using you," he went on. "I didn't comprehend how serious this holiday thing was for you, and had to push for what the company needed. So I tested you, yes, but with good intentions, as I said last night."

His expression confirmed his seriousness. The angles of his face were shadowed. He looked as if he hadn't slept, as if he also had tossed and turned, going over the events that had transpired and regretting not being honest earlier.

Was the elevator to become a confessional booth for issues that could be addressed right then in the secluded space, with no one else present? Personal confessions?

"I need time to process problems in my past," she said. "You've helped to make that clear, though I've known it all along. But because I might be vulnerable in my personal life doesn't equate to weakness in my professional ethics. It's just one thing that I need to deal with. Don't you have something you'd like to leave behind, even though it might be tough?"

"Yes," he said then added, "I'm sure everyone has something like that to face."

"It's easier when you have a family to back you up, though," she said. "As well as enough money to buy a company where you can set your own rules."

He took his time before responding. "There is a lot of risk involved with these investments. Not to mention stress," he said. "This has been an extraordinary few days, and I'll say one more time that I don't want the company to lose you. Will you agree to stay after all is said and done? Will knowing you have your job help with whatever it is you're going to do this week?"

Kim shook her head to hide the fact that the rest of her shook, as well. She felt something for this man, but wasn't sure what. The sensations had come on too quickly, were too intense and all-consuming. Their relationship had started with anger and ended with heat.

Last night had been over the top, for as long as it lasted. Monroe's body, his attention and his talents had caught her up, making her forget everything else that stood between them. But those moments of free fall had been ruined, and now she felt unsettled. The simplicity of an emotion like anger no longer fit or covered the situation. She wasn't sure what did.

She lifted her gaze to the level of his chin. "I'm sorry I said those things in front of your mother. That was inexcusable."

"I think my mother liked you. She called you feisty."

Kim blinked slowly to block out the scene.

"We don't have to talk now," he said. "Do whatever you need to do to fix what you have going on. Just don't count me as another problem to face, okay?"

"Are you offering to forget about the contract?"

"I can't forget it in a potential vice president. I know you understand that, and that I have to do what's best for the agency."

"What is it you want, then? Friendship?"

"Yes, if that's what it takes to keep you here. And no if I'm being completely truthful."

Kim's gaze rose higher. She didn't want to be his friend, either, though that might not have been possible anyway, given the intensity of their connection. Despite trying to repress her feelings, she imagined what his hands would again feel like on her bare back, and how his lips might again sweep her away if she and Monroe dared to allow the sparks between them to dictate their future actions.

Kissing him last night had seemed right. In his arms nothing else had existed for a while, beyond two flames merging.

Now…

Now they were embarrassed and taken aback by their behavior, and he wanted to mend the situation.

"We are having the party," he said. "It's my family's holiday celebration. I thought you should know that we're going to utilize all the ideas you and I talked about in the bar, and more. You don't have to be a part of planning, Kim, but I'd like you to attend."

"As your disgruntled employee whose covert nickname is Scrooge?"

"As my guest."

"I can't commit to that right now."

"Then you can give me your answer later. Maybe after a couple days off, you'll accept."

"Besides, I couldn't possibly be welcome after your mother witnessed the drama in your office," Kim said.

"On the contrary, my family thrives on drama. Trust me, you'd fit right in."

Kim fisted her hands, ready to get away from him and the things still left unsaid. Confusion reigned. She wanted to take a step forward, yet she couldn't allow it. She wanted to forget the past, but that past remained tied to her by a few tenacious threads. Relationship avoidance was one of them.

People got hurt if they fell hard and heaped love on one another, only to eventually have that love lost. Depression sometimes took over a lovesick soul. She had seen it happen firsthand.

She might like Monroe if she allowed herself to. She might have been able to love him someday, had the situation been different and she met him elsewhere.

"I'll send you the details," he said, bringing her out of her thoughts.

"You have a habit of refusing to take no for an answer," she said softly.

"Only where it concerns me personally, and I feel as though I have a stake in the outcome."

Of course, by personal, he was talking about his business, not about her. She had to keep that in mind. Monroe had to do what was best for the agency. His agency. Inviting her to the party was a final parting shot before sending her back to her cubicle.

He added, "If keeping you means hands-off, then that's the way it will be. However, I'm not lying to you when I say that I'd like to kiss you right now. Hell, I'd like to do much more than that, and take up where we left off last night. I will also tell you this, Kim. I have never invited a woman to my parents' home. You'd be the first. My guest. Night of fun. Truce in place."

She didn't have time to reply, and wasn't sure how to, anyway. The door opened with a whooshing sound. A wave of cooler air swirled around them. Kim didn't move until the doors started to close again and Monroe stepped in the way, a move that brought him closer to her and ensured that she had to touch him when she left the elevator.

Kim's motionless body brimmed with longing for the man she should be wary of. He was the boss, and she fully comprehended his problem with her. If getting the most out of the agency meant having management that oversaw every aspect of it, she was not that candidate.

Because she understood that, she also realized that Chaz Monroe wasn't the bad guy here, after all. She was disappointed about the job, but her anger with him had been misplaced.

The doors started to close, pushing at Monroe's wide shoulders. As she brushed past him, her left arm touched his. The charge that careened through her was powerful enough to bring on a gasp. The urge to turn to him, get close to him, walk right into the circle of his arms, was so strong, she stiffened. And in her peripheral vision, she watched his hands mirror hers, fisting so that he wouldn't catch her, change his mind and throw her against the gleaming metal.

And how she wanted him to do that, in spite of everything.

She paused close enough to him to feel his breath on her

forehead. Close enough that all she had to do was look up, and her lips would be within reach of his. The sensations running through her were blatant reminders that she really did feel something for this man.

"It should be easy to agree." Her voice caught. She sought his eyes, her pulse thudding hard. "When doing so might solve everything for a while."

"Maybe you will come to the party as a start toward a mutually beneficial future," he said. "I'm rooting for that."

He didn't grab her or kiss her, though Kim felt the pressure of that imaginary kiss as if he had overpowered her completely. She nearly backpedaled into the tiny space to make sure he did; almost asked him for a repeat of the mindless hunger that every cell in her body craved.

But Monroe moved out of the way, holding the door with one hand so that she could leave the elevator without further contact that would have spoken volumes about what they wanted to do to each other.

She had no alternative but to go.

Once she had passed him, Monroe stepped back inside and smiled at her earnestly, devastatingly, tiredly, as the elevator doors closed and the contraption took him from her, leaving her standing in the hallway.

Dozens of employees went about their business all around her, doing their jobs, unaware of the turmoil roiling through Kim that for one more brief moment made her need a wall for support.

# Ten

Kim stood on the sidewalk, staring at the house. In the late-afternoon sun, the two-story brick structure had a forlorn appearance. Not shabby, exactly, but uncared for, unkempt.

Dark windows punctuated the 1940s brick cottage. On the front porch sat a collection of empty clay pots that had once contained pink geraniums to brighten the place. The small lawn was neatly trimmed, and a concrete walkway had been swept clear of debris. She'd seen to that by hiring a neighbor kid, who had taken the job seriously, though not once in the past six months had she thought to check.

"Welcome home, Kim," she said to herself.

She picked up her small suitcase. Though the house in New Jersey was merely a half an hour's train ride from her apartment, she planned to stay during her vacation.

It was several minutes before she took the first step up that walkway. Kim had to consciously remember that times here hadn't always been dark, and that angst hadn't always ruled the space between those walls. There had been good times. Fun times. Lighter moments. She had loved her mother, doted on her mother, until very near to the end when others took over the daily routine. Her mother had loved her back, to the best of her ability. It was just that her mother must have loved the husband that had long ago disappeared, more.

The windows, devoid of holiday trappings, were not welcoming. The blinds were drawn to keep out the world, and possibly to keep the old darkness contained.

Kim set her shoulders. This trip home was about coming to terms with those moments of darkness and banishing them for good. Harboring guilt about the past was unreasonable, unhealthy and getting in the way of living her life the way she wanted to.

It wasn't Monroe's fault that this confrontation had come up. She had meant to take care of this ages ago.

She wished now that she'd taken Brenda up on her offer of company. Having a friend along would have been preferable to facing some ghosts solo. But she was a woman now, no longer an impressionable child. She'd inform this house and its ghosts of her plans to let in the light and dust away cobwebs. Her presence might reinforce the good times.

*If Monroe wanted a hassle-free associate, he'll soon have one,* she thought as she blinked slowly and gritted her teeth. Then she headed up the walkway, determined to see this housewarming through, trying hard to keep her thoughts from turning to charming Chaz Monroe, and finding that task way too difficult.

Chaz could not sit down. He paced his office, stopping now and then to gaze out the window. Each time he did, he noted as many holiday details on the street below as he could from this height, and also took stock of the clouds rolling in to ease the transition from evening to night.

Each detail brought Kim to mind with the heft of a full mental takeover.

He had picked up the phone twice in the past fifteen minutes to call her, or Brenda Chang, or damn it, anyone else who knew Kim. Deep down inside him was a feeling of emptiness, of being lost and cast adrift.

He had rudely passed Alice without a word on his way to the water cooler not half an hour ago, and that had not gone down well with Alice. She had ignored him ever since.

He knew all too well the word Rory would have used for this current agitated state. *Whipped.*

Did that describe him, at this point, and the sensation of being helpless to fix things in light of Kim's fast exit?

He was acting as if she had become an obsession, when there were plenty of other women in New York, and plenty of years to find them. McKinley, with her obstinate refusal to meet his terms, was a pain in his backside.

He kept telling himself that, over and over.

In all fairness, though, she had confessed to having problems and had spoken honestly about the possibility of facing them. So, what did that make him for wishing she'd hurry up and do so, when he now knew a few of the reasons that might have contributed to how messed up she felt this time of year? Sarah Summers had been thorough with the few details she dug up for him.

Kim was alone. He sympathized with her lack of family. The Monroes were a tight clan. His mother and father were together after forty years of marriage, with a loving relationship still going strong. His sister, Shannon, had found her guy after her first year at Harvard and settled down with a ring on her finger by the time of her graduation last year. Rory was…Rory.

His family life wasn't perfect. Whose was? Yet they were supportive in the fierceness of their loyalty to each other. Their time together, though rare these days, was always a welcome delight.

What if, like Kim, he had no family? No brothers or sisters. No mother and father to use for backup. Taking that further, what if after working hard to gain traction in his career, some newcomer suddenly threatened to derail that career?

He leaned against the windowsill, deep in thought. Kim's father was probably alive, but lost to her. The man had filed for divorce when she was a kid. Intel said that Kim's mother had gone in and out of hospitals after the divorce, until Deborah McKinley passed away earlier this year. Had those things—the divorce and being left by her husband—been the cause of Kim's mother's prolonged illness?

That would have been hard enough to take, but nothing he had found explained why this holiday in particular got to Kim, and how it got her down. He needed to know about this. He had to understand what lay at the root of her dislike for the season. If as an only child, things had been bad with her mother, had some of her mother's depression rubbed off on Kim in ways that continued to show up?

With a quick glance at his watch, Chaz hustled out of the office, grabbing his jacket from the chair by the door. There was only one person who could help him out by filling in a few more blanks. He had to persuade Brenda to talk, knowing her to be Kim's best friend, and that it wouldn't be easy.

Kim climbed the stairs to her old bedroom and dropped her bag on the floor. The room smelled stale. Dust covered every available surface. The really scary thing was how nothing else had changed. Her bedroom remained exactly the same after all this time, yet another example of her late mother's need for pattern and constancy.

"I refuse to feel bad about the state of the place. I do not live here anymore."

She heard no answering voice in the empty house, only silence. The place felt cold. Outside temperatures had plummeted, and the inside of the house matched.

"Next stop, the furnace." She spoke out loud to ward off the silence.

On her way downstairs, she passed her mother's room. The door was closed, and she left it that way, preferring comfort to memory at the moment, and believing her recent mental adjustments to be good signs of being on the road to recovery.

"Thermostat up. Check."

To her relief, the furnace kicked on. She took this as another good omen, and headed for the kitchen, which would have been in pristine condition, except for the layer of dust.

Glad now that she hadn't turned off the electricity or gas, Kim took one good glance at the room where she and her mother had cooked and then dined at the small square table against the wall, preferring the warm kitchen to the formal dining room.

She opened a few cupboards and the refrigerator then headed upstairs for her purse. Kitchens needed to be stocked, and her stomach hadn't stopped growling. She couldn't recall the last time she'd eaten, or sat down for a meal. The hours spent in her apartment always seemed rushed, with lots of takeout Chinese.

She used to like to cook. Her mother, during her good spells, had taught her. Baking became her favorite, though those cookies she dumped last night had been her first foray into trying out those skills in years. *Christmas cookies...*

Well, she had plenty of time now to explore her talents. With a few days off, she'd get back in the groove and whip up something good. A roast, maybe, with vegetables. She'd clean up the house and make it sparkle before putting it up for sale with the hope that some family might be happier here than she and her mother were. Like most people, she supposed houses needed love and attention in order to feel homey. She'd see to that.

But first, groceries.

She'd change her clothes, walk to the market a block over, and be back before dark if she hustled. There'd be time to thoroughly clean the kitchen after she got something in the oven. She would have to learn to slow down in measured increments. She felt all riled up. She wasn't used to off-time from work, though her plan to fix up the house would occupy her for a while.

Plus, she was happy to note, she hadn't thought about

Monroe much in the last ten minutes. That also meant
headway.

*Damn his handsome hide.* She'd see to it that running
away from Chaz Monroe would turn out to be produc-
tive....

"Brenda?"

She did a slow rotation in her chair and looked at Chaz
warily.

"You're working late," he said.

"If this job was nine to five, Mr. Monroe, maybe I'd
have time for a date."

Alice had been right about Brenda, who obviously
shared none of Kim's abhorrence of the season. A minia-
ture Christmas tree sat on her desk, wrapped with blinking
lights and tiny ornaments. Tinsel garlands hung between
two bookshelves. The cubicle retained a faint smell of evergreen.

Chaz waved a hand at the tree. "Does she come in here?"

"Not this time of year." Brenda did not pretend to mis-
understand whom he was talking about.

"You don't push your ideas on her?"

"She's my friend and has a right to her own opinions."

Chaz sat on the edge of her desk, looking at the wall
separating Kim's cubicle from this one.

"You seem to be worried about her," Brenda said.

"Aren't you?"

She eyed him as if sizing him up. "She's a big girl and
will get on with her life as she sees fit."

"She's sad, I think."

Brenda did not respond to his diagnosis of Kim's state
of mind.

"Do you know what problems she has with the holiday,
Brenda?" he asked.

"Sorry, can't talk about that. I promised."

"Yet I get the impression you'd like to help her somehow."

Brenda sighed. "Of course I'd like to help her out of the current mess she's in. I'm not insensitive to what's going on."

"But you believe that nothing, other than her job here, is my business?"

"That's right. I'm sorry."

Chaz stood up. "Fair enough. Can you tell me something, though, that might help? Anything?"

"I doubt it. So will you fire me for protecting my friend's privacy?"

"Only if I was the monster everyone seems to think I am."

"Are you saying you're not?"

He smiled. "I'm pretty hopeful that Kim might be the only one who thinks so."

"Yet you want more information from me so that you can do what?"

"Whittle away at her resolve," he replied.

"Which part of that resolve? The contract, or staying away from you?"

"I like her," Chaz said. "More than I should."

Brenda took a beat to think that over. "What makes you think whittling can work?"

"Because of something I just recalled about her apartment last night that I can't forget."

"What?"

"Last night her apartment smelled like cookies."

Brenda waved a hand in the air to dismiss the remark. "That tells you something, how?"

"Sugar cookies hold a fragrance unique to this holiday in particular," he said. "I grew up with that smell. It's unmistakable and always makes my mouth water. Sugar cookies are a Christmas staple. Even old Claus himself can't resist them."

Brenda took another minute to reply. Chaz watched her mull that information over. "Could have been something else, and you are mistaken," she suggested. "Could have been chocolate chip."

"I'm not wrong about that one thing," he said. "She had baked those cookies pretty near to Christmas. My question for you is if that's usual, and if Kim bakes all the time?"

Brenda's brow creased. Chaz noted how much she hated answering that question.

"I've never known her to bake anything," she admitted.

He nodded and asked the other question plaguing him. "Then how is it that a person who shuns the season and all of its trappings would bake Christmas cookies, especially after having it out with her boss about a holiday clause in her contract?"

Brenda, Chaz realized, was not at a loss. Rebounding from the cookie inquisition, she said, "If you're right about the cookies, it means she's trying."

"Trying to what?"

"Move on."

"Regarding the holiday?"

"In regard to everything."

Chaz glanced again at the wall between the cubicles. "Thank you, Brenda. That's all I needed to know."

She stopped him with a hand on his arm. "It's not all you need to know, and I can't tell you the rest."

"I know about her mother," he said. "And also about her father leaving early on."

"Maybe you do, but the story goes much deeper than that for Kim."

"Yet you won't help me to understand what that story is."

"My lips are necessarily sealed."

"Nevertheless, it's possible that she might be attempting

to deal with change. In the elevator, she told me she wants to. You do think she is seriously open to trying?"

Brenda nodded tentatively. "I do. But you're pushing her, you know. There's a chance you'll push too far."

"I feel as though I need to get to the bottom of this. I'm not completely insensitive. I have feelings, too. I like her. I've admitted that. And I know how to sell a project."

"Kim's not a project. She's a person."

"Yes," he agreed. "A special one."

Brenda looked to the hallway. "I get that you like her, yet I'm not sure you should be poking around where you don't belong, or that your interest can speed things up."

"I can only try to make things better. I won't purposefully hurt her. That much I'll swear to you right now. Any time you want to jump in and help my cause, you'd be more than welcome."

Brenda dropped her hand.

"I suppose," Chaz said, "it might not be a good idea to tell Kim about this conversation. Knowing where your loyalty lies, I'm asking for your trust in the matter."

Brenda looked terribly conflicted when he left her. He heard her say behind him, "You have feelings, huh? I certainly hope you prove that."

# Eleven

An hour and a half after getting back from the market, the kitchen had filled with the delicious smell of a roast cooking. Pile a few carrots on, a cut-up potato and some broth, and the atmosphere of the house had already changed for the better. The place had started to feel lived in.

Kim wore an apron, which she figured officially earned her the title of Miss Homebody for the next few days. She had already scrubbed away at the layer of dust piled everywhere in the kitchen and dining room, and mopped the floors. Keeping busy was the key to kicking off this hiatus from her daily routine. She was used to being busy all the time. In advertising, there was little if any downtime because the mind had to constantly be on the move.

Wasn't there an old saying about idle hands?

She set the table for one and opened a bottle of wine to let it breathe, as the woman in the market had recommended. With no wineglasses in the house, she washed out a teacup and tried to recall when she had last dated. Thanksgiving week? Maybe nearer to Halloween? Could it have been as far back as Valentine's Day? She never went out after Thanksgiving, and tended not to look at men at all until after the New Year had rung in. Being anti-holiday had always been difficult to explain.

Clearly though, meeting Chaz Monroe brought home the fact that she'd been alone for too long. Being so very physically connected to him likely was the result of having saved herself from any kind of personal contact for a while. That's why her body and her raging hormones had been perfectly willing to allow Monroe's talented hands and mouth to take her over.

She might be flawed, but she was a woman, with a woman's needs. Monroe had made that all too obvious.

The cup rattled on the table when she set it down. *Monroe.* There he was again, in her thoughts, seeping through the cracks of her determination not to think about him.

Merely the idea of him set off physical alarms. Her neck began to tingle as if his lips touched her there in a soft, seductive nuzzle. Her back muscles tightened with the memory of the red dress's zipper inching down slowly to grant him access to her naked, heated skin.

There was something so damn sexy about a zipper.

She took hold of the back of the chair and tossed her head to negate those memories, tired of feeling torn by them and believing she was a freak. She refused to let all the pent-up emotion she'd withheld for so long come to a head before she'd spent one night in her mother's home.

"Facing this house has to be the first step," she said aloud to set that objective in stone. "If I can do this, I can tackle anything."

She got to work. When she had finished cleaning the dining room, she moved to the living room. Dusting, vacuuming, plumping pillows, she worked up a sweat. Finally satisfied that she'd done all she could for the moment to make the place habitable, she saw to her dinner.

Seated at the small table in the kitchen, she poured the wine. Without the talent to discern if it was good wine or not, she took a sip. "Not too bad, I guess, if alcohol is your thing."

Hell, if there was no one to talk to, she'd continue to talk to herself.

Dishing up the roast took seconds. Digging in took a little longer. Without anyone real to talk to, the kitchen seemed way too quiet. The clock on the wall no longer worked. There had never been a radio in the kitchen for comforting background noise—which might have set a good atmosphere for dinnertime conversation, and had never really turned out that way.

In contrast to the busy hallways and thin walls of her apartment building, the two-story house felt like a fortress of solitude, exemplified by the empty chair next to her. As Kim sat there with her uneaten dinner a pang of loneliness hit, accompanied by a wave of deep-seated sadness.

She had the power to fix this. She had to fix it by looking back logically. Her mother's decline was a lesson in how not to behave. Kim might have tossed some good guys with potential to the wayside because of a few deeply ingrained and very silly ideas about relationships.

If she didn't face her problems head-on, she'd never have anyone in her life. Being good at her job was one thing, and satisfying, but coming home to an empty house or an empty apartment night after night forever was a nightmare she had feared to confront.

She pictured her mother here, cooking dinner for one and eating in the quiet. The image broke her heart. The guilt she'd harbored for growing up and being away, for leaving her mother for school and work, plagued her all over again. She just hadn't been able to cope year after year with her mother's mental illness.

Kim lifted her chin. Raising her cup to the empty chair, she spoke with more confidence than she felt. "If things are going to change, we're going to have to break the spell."

The cup was halfway to her lips when a bell rang. Startled by the sound, Kim jumped to her feet.

*Doorbell?*

Her city sensibilities kicked in. Single women didn't answer the door unless they knew who stood on the other side. Buildings had doormen for that reason.

Other than Brenda, no one knew she was here. But, she reminded herself, this wasn't the city. This was a family neighborhood. Things were different here. Maybe the kid down the street had seen the lights and wanted payment in person for mowing the lawn.

With a glance through the small glass panel in the front door, Kim flipped on the porch light. She saw no one on the steps. Cautiously, she opened the door. Nobody was there. Her gaze dropped to the large cardboard box on the doorstep.

There had been a delivery, but it had to have been a mistake.

Stepping outside, looking around, she again glanced at the box. Her name was written on it, but there was no return address.

She took the box inside and carefully tore it open, then drew back after viewing the contents. The box contained several smaller boxes with see-through lids and big red bows. All of the boxes contained cookies. By the looks of things, every kind of cookie under the sun, including decorated Christmas trees.

It took her a moment to remember to breathe. Forgetting her mother was no longer there, Kim waited for the rant against the holidays to begin. A Christmas gift had been delivered to a house that didn't take kindly to such things. *Who would dare to deliver such a thing?* her mother would have shouted. *Who would allow items like that in their house?*

Of course, no rants came. Her mother's tirades were over. The walls hadn't fallen down because of the box on the living room floor. Her mother hadn't been raised from the grave by the pretty sugar-coated shapes.

Kim let out a breath and went back to the door for a second look outside. Cars went by. Two kids rode skateboards down the middle of the road. There was no one else in sight.

"Okay, then. It's an anonymous gift. A surprise."

Leaving the box on the floor, she headed to the kitchen. At the table, she sat down and picked up her fork, though jumbled thoughts prevented her from taking a bite of the roast, which was getting cold. Brenda wouldn't have delivered a package like that, thinking to help Kim's vow along. Brenda probably would have presented the box in person if it was to be an offering to the House of Christmas Doom. Besides, Bren didn't know about the secretly baked sugar cookies she'd dumped the night before.

If not Brenda, who had sent them?

She felt a chill on the back of her neck. Kim sat up straighter, not liking the idea that sprang to mind.

*Monroe?*

No. It couldn't be him.

She wasn't sure why his name had come up with regard to this box. He had no idea where she'd gone. However, Monroe might do such a thing if he knew where she was. She wouldn't put it past him to send his own version of a peace offering.

The tingle at the base of her neck returned, along with a fair amount of heat that wasn't in any way reasonable. The telltale flush creeping up her throat wasn't reasonable, either.

She couldn't allow herself to go there, to think about him, when already her forehead felt damp, and her hands were shaking. But accepting his gift would amount to another step in the right direction in her plan to tackle each problem that came up, and deal.

There wasn't any reason to close the box back up and put it outside. Letting it remain there, on the floor, was okay, but it did press home the fact that she was no longer bothered by one objective, but by two: how to face the holiday positively, and what to do about her boss.

Her stomach tightened, but not in a bad way.

Leaving her dinner untouched in the kitchen, Kim stood up. There was only one way Monroe could have found her, if in fact, he had.

"I'll get you for this, Bren," she muttered, heading up-stairs for her cell phone.

But she didn't call Brenda. Instead, she dialed the num-ber of the VP's office, wondering if she'd hang up if some-one answered this late, and what she planned to say if *he* picked up the phone.

He did.

"Monroe," he said in the way he had of making the sim-plest words sound provocative.

Kim didn't speak. She hadn't been prepared for her re-action to the deep richness of his voice. Her finger hovered over the button that would disconnect her from him even as her mind registered this kind of reaction as being silly. All she had to do was ask him if he'd sent the box, and the mystery would be over.

"You got the package?" he asked, somehow knowing she was on the line, obviously confident she'd respond posi-tively to his gift.

For the first time in her life, Kim felt at a loss.

*Hang up now,* she told herself. *I don't need this.*

"I found your mother's address and wanted to send you something," he said, as if they weren't having a one-sided conversation. "Everybody likes cookies. And I'm still hop-ing that you'll be staying on at the agency."

"So you sent a bribe?" she managed to say, realizing only then that he'd have access to her files and her old address, and that Brenda might not have been a traitor.

"You do know they're Christmas cookies?" she added.

"I had them delivered to you by courier because I thought returning to your former home with your mother gone might make you sad, and that you might need cheer-ing up."

That made Kim hesitate. He might or might not have known about the depth of her aversion to this holiday, but he did know about her mother's passing. He hadn't sent this package to distress her further, but with hopes of making her happy. The gift was kind of personal. He had chosen it himself.

Kim wasn't sure how to take that. She did feel a ridiculous amount of anxiety—or maybe it was excitement—over the thought of Monroe taking the time to buy her a gift and get that gift to her not long after their conversation in the elevator.

Uncertain, she said, slightly breathlessly, "Thank you."

It was his turn to hesitate. She heard him breathing, and she also fought for each breath taken. The electricity in their connection felt like tiny jabs of lightning piercing her skin. Their chemistry was palpable, even this far apart.

"Are you okay?" he asked, sounding concerned.

"I'm fine," she lied.

"The gift didn't offend you, I hope? I swear that wasn't my intention."

"Not anymore."

"Good." Relief lowered his voice. "The red bows made me think of you in the red dress. You caused quite a stir in that dress, you know."

"Are you going to talk dirty to me on the phone?" she asked, at a loss for keeping the conversation on a serious track.

He laughed, and the sound rippled through her like a warm, sunny breeze. She loved that laugh. It made her feel lighter and not so alone. It made her want to laugh with him, and at herself for being so serious.

Maybe Monroe wasn't so full of himself after all.

Maybe she was.

Chances were that they could at least be friends if she allowed it.

"Actually," he said, "it's not late, and I wondered if you'd invite me over to eat some of the cookies."

"I'm pretty sure that wouldn't be a good idea."

She was positive that having him over wouldn't be a good idea. With a connection this strong, being in the same room with Monroe might lead to another situation she'd regret. This was her mother's home. A man of interest had no place here until she got her act together and banished the multiple years of gloom.

"I can bring dinner," he said. "No strings, just dinner."

"Thanks, but I've made dinner."

"Made dinner?" he repeated. "You cook?"

The astonishment in his sexy voice ruffled her ego.

"As a matter of fact, I do a lot of things you don't know about, and rather well, I might add," she said.

"I don't get much home cooking these days. Of course, you've probably already eaten, and you're busy getting a start on that vacation. So, all right. I didn't mean to pry any further into your affairs."

"Of course you did," she said.

"Well, yes, I guess I did…though I respect your right to turn my company down."

"Not your company, necessarily. Just you."

"Ouch. Well then, enjoy your time off. I hope those cookies bring you some happiness, too. I'd like to think they could, anyway."

Not knowing how to respond to the attention, Kim muttered "Thank you" again, and let it go at that. After reluctantly disconnecting, she immediately wished she hadn't. Monroe's voice and the interruption caused by the arrival of his gift had made the empty house almost seem livable for a change.

She felt excited—for no reason at all.

The phone remained in her hand for several more seconds before she made an SOS call to Brenda.

"Help," she said when her friend answered. "He's at it again, and I'm afraid I might be weakening."

# Twelve

"Just to be clear," Brenda said, "when you say you're weakening, are we talking about the jolly guy in the red suit, or our gorgeous, if rather nosy, new boss?"

"Both," Kim said, her skin prickling with a new kind of anxiousness.

"Shall I come over?"

"No."

"You know, it isn't always a bad thing to have temporary insanity, and for you that might mean letting go of preconceived notions about liking a man."

"He sent me a gift."

"Who did?"

"Monroe sent a package. Here. Tonight."

Brenda's pause amounted to a dead line. "Please tell me there were diamonds involved, as in a bracelet or necklace, because otherwise what would constitute a proper apology for behaving like a cad in your apartment last night, and leading you astray about the job?"

"Cookies. He sent a box of cookies," Kim said.

"Doesn't work for me, Kim. That's much too benign for a sincere apology. Do you want me to come over there and help you break those cookies into tiny pieces?"

"I'd like your idea on what to do about *him*."

"I'm honored by your confidence in my advice, Kim, but honestly, I'm not sure about this."

"Brenda!"

"Well, okay. In this case, I'd probably note that Monroe sent you his version of an earnest apology."

"He said he hoped they made me happy."

"You talked to him?"

"I thanked him on the phone."

"I see. Well, it's probably okay, I'm thinking. Cookies, though delicious, aren't truly personal. They're not like lingerie, so you can probably ignore this and move on if you choose to."

"Thing is..." Kim didn't finish the sentence. She really felt confused.

"Thing is, a box from Monroe might actually help you in this self-imposed crisis?" Brenda observed, picking up on Kim's thought pattern.

"Yes." Kim silently applauded Brenda for understanding the pros and pitfalls of the situation.

"Then it's a win-win, Kim," Brenda concluded. "He was being nice, and you've thanked him. Now you can eat those things and make more progress on your objective behind going home. Did you actually open the box?"

"I did."

"How did that make you feel?"

"Scared."

"I do kind of get that, but will ask this question, anyway. Why? Why were you scared?"

"It's my mother's house, Bren. Feeling good here seems strange. Holiday gifts were taboo, sacrilege."

"Were taboo, but not anymore. That stuff happened when your mom was alive, but she's gone, and you've gone home to change and rearrange your attitude about things. There's not one person on the planet to stop you from accomplishing that goal, except yourself."

"Right." Kim sighed. "Except for me."

After an audible breath, Brenda asked, "Are they from a decent bakery?"

"Becons, by the park."

"Well, you can be thankful he has good taste. Take them out of the box. Have some for dinner. Sweets always make us feel good, right?"

This was good advice and another necessary push along a new path. She wasn't a child in need of a lesson, though Kim felt like one every time she entered this house. In her own world, she took charge. In her own world, she was successful and happy enough...if there was such a thing as being happy *enough*.

"I'm flawed, Bren, and I don't want other people to find out. One in particular."

"Because you care what he thinks?"

"I think I do."

"So what's stopping you from dropping the *I think* part of that?"

Brenda spoke again over Kim's thoughtful pause. "I was heading to the bar with the art guys to catch up on gossip, but I can grab the next train if you need me. Say the word and I'll be on that train."

"No. I'm okay. Thanks for the pep talk."

"No problem. Sending you hugs over the ether. Good luck with the caloric fallout, Kimmy."

"Have an appletini for me, Bren."

"Heck, it has been a very long day, so I might have two."

Disconnecting, Kim glanced around, inwardly reciting the words Brenda had offered. There was no one to stop her from attaining her objective for coming here, but herself.

*Time to get on with things.*

The old bathroom in the hallway seemed big and drafty after the tiny one in her apartment, but the shower still worked, and she had brought along clean towels. She took her time under the spray of water, trying not to think about how Monroe had nearly succeeded in getting her naked.

She scrubbed her back hard, sloughing off the sensation of his hands on her skin, erasing the memory of his fingers exploring with a blistering heat...but not quite ridding herself of those sensations.

In her determination not to think of him, she was doing a

lousy job. In fact, she failed miserably. In Monroe's strong arms, and for a few brief, sizzling moments, she had been someone else. She had let him in. For the first time, she hadn't allowed her past to influence her actions.

She did like Chaz Monroe.

She'd been hot and bothered since that first glimpse of him in his office. Her body responded favorably each time he neared, as if her nervous system needed to bypass her damaged, overworked brain, and get to the good part.

Fact was, she had the hots for her boss and wished he was in the shower with her, working his magic right that minute. Heck, if she was that far gone, was she so severely damaged that she'd refuse to accept his offer of a truce?

Yes. Because liking him and pursuing a liaison would surely mean professional suicide eventually, as she had told him. And she had nothing without her job.

In her bedroom, she removed clothes from her bag and shook them out. She pulled on a pair of well-worn sweatpants and fingered a silky blue camisole as she drew it over her head, knowing Monroe would also have liked its texture and color. Covering that with a loose wool cardigan sweater, gathering her hair into a ponytail, she headed downstairs in her bare feet.

The house had warmed up considerably now that the old heater hummed. She turned on all the lights, hesitating at each switch to think about how Monroe seemed to like her, too. Not all had to be lost in this situation, if she looked on the bright side. He was willing to overlook the clause in her contract if she stayed in her cubicle. He just couldn't promote her or send her any more gifts if she remained an employee.

She might or might not be able to deal with that.

Circling back to the living room, she stared at the floor. *Step one: take the cookies out of the box. Eat one, or ten. It will be a good thing, a helpful thing.*

Kneeling next to the box, she lifted out the first smaller box, noting again that lightning did not strike. The walls did not fall down.

She lifted out another container and went back in memory to the times as a child when she had wished for a gift like this.

"It's okay. Therapy."

After she had unpacked all four-dozen cookies, she got to her feet. The first step was working. Some of her guilt had already fled, chased away by things that weren't really magical at all, but at the moment seemed magical to her.

She was smiling.

"What if I had invited him to dinner?" she said aloud. "Wouldn't that hurry things along?"

No reply came. No argument or lament from the house's ghosts. She was free now to make her own choices, and had been for some time. Suddenly, she understood that fully.

When her phone rang, Kim took the stairs two at a time, figuring that Brenda would be checking in. She plopped down on the bed. "Bren, guess what?"

A low-pitched masculine voice said, "Are you sure you won't change your mind and invite me over if I say please and categorically deny being a stalker, providing references upon request?"

*Monroe.* Her heart began to thud inside her chest. Her throat tightened. How persistent was he going to be? And why wasn't she displeased?

"I'm nowhere near where you are, as you already know, having sent the package," Kim said.

"You'd see me otherwise?"

"No," she lied again, ill-equipped to handle what he was suggesting. Admittedly, the house might have been brighter already, though it remained too quiet. More cleaning would only get her so far in terms of occupying her time. A whole night stretched in front of her, with far too many hours to fill.

She missed her cozy apartment.

Clearly, Monroe's gift had shocked her into some kind of middle ground where she might consider seeing him.

If she did, she'd find out what he really wanted from her. She could stand her ground and face him; she'd show him that she was taking charge of her life in all situations, and that she would make up her own mind about her future. In that light, seeing Monroe might be a good idea.

"Kim? You there?"

It was rotten how her pulse jumped after hearing his voice, and how the hand holding the phone trembled, especially when only five minutes before she'd made up her mind to stand firm against the potency of his allure.

"Well, maybe. If you were closer," she said, not really having to worry about that remark since she was no longer in the city.

There was a knock on the front door.

"You'll have to excuse me. Someone is at the door," Kim said. "I have to go."

"Take me with you, in case it's someone you don't want to see," Monroe said. "Be on the safe side."

Kim ran back downstairs, turned on the porch light and looked through the glass. She whirled with her back to the door and leaned against it, raising the phone.

"What is it?" he whispered in her ear.

But she could not speak.

Outside, on her porch, was a Christmas tree, its shape unmistakable.

"Did you send a tree?" she demanded, her voice faint, her heart hammering.

"I did not, in fact, send the tree," Monroe replied.

*Do not open the door,* Kim's inner lecturer told her.

*It's too much, too soon.*

Placing a hand on the knob, she waited out several racing heartbeats. An idea came to her, along with a sudden waft of familiar heat. She said into the phone, "I suppose if I open this door, someone will be holding that tree?"

"Someone who could possibly contract pneumonia from standing in the cold," Monroe said. "Plus, I did get an invitation, sort of. I am in the area, as it turns out."

Kim lowered the phone and opened the door. Monroe stood there, all right, holding the tree. The sight registered as surreal.

"Semantics," he clarified. "I didn't send the tree, I *brought* it."

Before Kim knew what was happening, she was up tight against him, listening to the muffled crash of the tree falling to the porch floorboards as she pressed her mouth to his.

# Thirteen

Kim McKinley was a frigging enigma. But who had the time or inclination to put on the brakes?

The woman who occupied every waking thought was in his arms, at least for the next minute or two, until her sanity returned. And though he had planned on talking to her and keeping a discreet distance, his hunger came raging back from where logic had stored it, overpowering his struggle to comprehend the situation.

What else could he do except let himself go?

The meeting of their mouths was intense, and like food for the starving. She welcomed his touch, his tongue, his strength, seemingly determined to have a replay of the night before, and to see this through. Whatever *this* was to her.

She did not want the kiss to stop, and made that quite clear. But she was tense. When his arms tightened around her, she breathed out a sound of distress.

He loosened his grip, moving his hands to her rib cage, waiting to see if she'd repeat the sound. She didn't. Through the sweater, he caught a feel of something slick, like a silky second skin. The thought of Kim's body again sheathed in the filmy material was a deal breaker in terms of his vow to keep his distance.

A big-time vow breaker.

Deepening the feverish kiss, then easing up, he stroked her softly, almost tenderly, with a desire to discover every part of the body he had dreamed about. Her hips molded to his. Her back arched each time his hands moved. She clung to his shoulders. Her breasts pressed against his chest. She was going for this. There was nothing to impede the forward momentum of this reunion.

*Well, okay.*

Chaz backed her up, through the open doorway. As he turned her to the wall, the impact of their moving bodies slammed the door. The sound seemed to reverberate through Kim, as though she'd felt a chill wind. A shiver ran through her. Her mouth slackened. Her hands were suddenly motionless.

*Hot and cold...*

*Seriously?*

The dichotomy of those temperatures ran through his mind with the fury of a wildfire. Chaz drew back far enough to see Kim's face in the dim light of an overhead entryway lamp. As before, when Brenda Chang's voice had driven a wedge between them, her face paled. Did she regret her reaction to him already? Was she nothing but a tease? Damn it, what just happened? He was all fired up.

"What is it?" he asked. "What's going on?"

Her eyes were wide and unseeing. He cradled her face with both hands and spoke again. "Kim? Look at me."

The hazel eyes, more green than brown, refocused.

"It's okay," he said. "I didn't come here to do that. We don't have to do anything but talk. See?"

He dropped his hands and stepped back. "You sounded lonely on the phone. I'll go if you ask me to, though I'd like to stay."

She shook her head. "It's just that… It's just that there hasn't been any company in this house for as long as I can remember. Certainly never a man. I felt…"

"I can be good company when I put my mind to it," he said when she didn't finish. "So what do you say we make up for lost time?"

"Yes." She smiled, though she looked wary. "Okay."

He glanced past her at the living room and withheld a frown. This wasn't like any room he had imagined her in, and nothing like what he'd seen of her apartment. This room didn't reflect her personality at all…unless of course she actually had a split down the middle.

The place wasn't drab, really, but very close to it. There were faded floral curtains, a beige cushioned sofa, and hardwood floors covered by rugs. The musty smell hinted at the house having been closed up for some time, though he also caught a whiff of a cleaning product.

On the floor sat the box he had sent. Kim had looked at the contents, at least. She'd had her hands on that box.

He wanted her hands back on him, but had to play nice and see how far he got with that idea. His plan was to break the news no one else yet knew—about his intention to turn over the agency to a new owner in the near future. Once the finances were settled in the black zone, he'd be gone. If he told Kim about this, and she realized she would still have a shot at the job she coveted, they might have a chance to explore the heat building up each time they came into contact with each other.

It wasn't the first time he'd thought about that. He just had to wait for the right time to spring it on her.

"Shall we start by bringing in the tree?" he asked. "I feel sort of sorry for it out there."

He took her silence for a no. Maybe she wasn't ready for another surprise gift.

"Conversation would also be nice," he suggested. "How about if I start, and clear the air?"

Her eyes remained on him in such a way that he wanted to kiss her again and bypass the rest of what kept them apart. Even her serious expression was sexy. As for her killer body…well, that was the icing on the cake he couldn't yet have a bite of.

"I'm here because I didn't want to leave things the way they were," he said. "Our confessions in the elevator only whetted my appetite for truthfulness. I thought by coming here, we could patch things up and move forward at a faster pace. If you're game, that is."

"Is there a rush?" she asked, tilting her head, showing off more of her long, bare, graceful neck.

"I thought so," he replied, stunned at how that stretch of pale skin affected him. "And now that I see you here, in this place, I'm not so sure this is a good location for you to spend your vacation time."

She didn't argue with his assessment. "This is a sad house."

"Does that mean you have to be sad in it?"

"It's hard to change the past, but I'm here to try."

"Yes, I suppose change is difficult. You might start by inviting me in. We could liven up the place for an hour or two."

She raised an eyebrow. "Do you recognize the word *pushy?*"

Chaz raised his hands. "How about if we start over and I go outside and knock, and you don't accost me wickedly this time when you open the door?"

She made a face. He had to wonder how deep her inner pressures went for her to embrace so many different emotions in the span of a few minutes.

This was indeed a sad house, but houses were built of wood and plaster, and possessed no souls. Though the temperature was warm inside, the room had an empty, cool feel. Already, after a few hours here, Kim looked like a different person, a sadder version, and his protective hackles had gone up.

Was he back to being a fool for wanting what he might never have? Why would he desire her when she was so confusing most of the time?

"Or you could ask me to take off my coat and sit down." He gestured to the sofa. "And we could try to behave like civilized people."

"Be my guest," she said, stepping aside.

Chaz tossed his coat on a chair and sat down on the couch, relieved to have gotten this far and wondering how she could look as good in sweats as she did all dolled up for work. He liked the fact that Kim seemed less formidable in this kind of casual wear, and in her bare feet. He liked her hair swept back in a ponytail, and felt an urge to pull strands loose to run between his fingers.

"Would you like something to drink?" She remained by the door. "I've got wine in teacups. I'm thinking of starting a new fad at wine bars. Merlot in chipped china. Very snazzy."

Chaz smiled. "All right. I'll try that. Can I help?"

"Let's confine you to one room at a time," she replied with a slight smile.

Kim seemed to have thawed again, though he had a feeling she might run out the back door and leave him there. Relief came when he heard her closing cupboard doors in the next room.

He didn't bother to check out more of his surroundings, noting only that there were no pictures, either on the walls or in frames set on the end tables. Not one photo of Kim existed in this room, whereas in his parents' home, every surface held a snapshot or two chronicling the family through the years.

The lack of personal touches here bothered him. After seeing a small portion of her apartment in the city, albeit in the dark, Kim's taste ran to modern. No clutter. Sleek lines, with lots of leather. That kind of decor suited her much better. This was old stuff, and quite depressing.

Clinking sounds brought his gaze to the kitchen doorway. Kim hadn't been kidding about the cups. She appeared carrying two, and handed him one without allowing her fingers to touch his in the transfer. She moved his coat and sat in the chair opposite him with her legs curled under her.

Very much like a kid. Also like a seductive siren with no idea of how hot she really was.

Several deep breaths were necessary before Chaz's first sip of wine. He eyed her over the rim. "Hate to tell you this, Kim, but even our agency couldn't sell your new wine in china fad to the public."

She smiled earnestly, he thought, and the smile lit up her face. "Something about the textures being wrong," she agreed. "Porcelain adds a taste of its own."

"What's the wine?"

"I've no idea. It was recommended by the local grocer."

Chaz chuckled and took another sip before setting the cup on the coffee table. He folded his hands in his lap to keep himself from reaching for the woman who had the ability to drive him mad with desire.

"How long has it been since you lived here?" he asked.

"A couple years. I stayed as long as I could and until…" She let whatever she had been about to say go, and started over. "Nothing has changed in here since I was a kid. I'm going to fix it up to sell. There will be a lot of work to get it ready."

"That's why you're here?"

"Partially."

"The other part?"

"Confronting ghosts."

It was a reply Chaz hadn't anticipated. His smile faltered as he watched Kim slip a silky aqua-blue strap back over her shoulder, beneath the sweater, where it stayed for a few seconds before falling back down. *Treacherous little strap.* His eyes strayed to her breasts, their contour visible through the slinky blue-green silk. She wasn't dressed for ghost hunting, but for cuddling.

And he had to stop thinking about that.

Whether or not she noticed his appreciative gaze, Kim pulled the soft sweater around her, which was a good move, and helped him to avoid more thoughts about how smooth her skin was, and where touching it might lead.

Still, as he saw it now, they were faced with a quandary. He was, anyway. Perfume wafted in the air he had to breathe. Kim's body taunted him from behind its cloth barrier. His reaction to these things were proof positive that he couldn't work in the same building with her after this. Maybe not even in the same city.

But he had started this by asking for a night of sharing confidences, and by showing up on her doorstep. Confidences and sex didn't necessarily go together.

He wanted her, but so what?

"Are we past the tape recorder duel?" he asked.

"Are we still negotiating?" she countered. "Is that the reason for the gifts?"

He shook his head. "No. Since we're being honest, I'll admit again to feeling uneasy about the way things have gone down between us. As I mentioned, our chat in the elevator didn't ease my mind much as to what to do."

"Why?"

"I don't honestly know. I wish I did."

"Are you sorry about the kiss in my doorway?" she asked.

"No." He zeroed in on her eyes. "Are you?"

"Not really."

Chaz swiped at the prickle on the back of his neck that was a warning signal to either get out of there with his masculinity intact, or get on with things. Talking about emotions wasn't listed in his personal portfolio of things he liked to do best. He was pretty sure no guy excelled at this kind of thing.

"I do hope you don't welcome everybody like that, though," he said in a teasing tone.

Kim shrugged. "How do you suppose I've kept my clients so happy?"

Chaz grinned before remembering her comments about sleeping her way to the top.

"Shall we move on to something else?" he suggested.

"I don't think so. Part of my healing process is to deal. So I'm going to tell you what you've wanted to know, and fulfill your objective for showing up here tonight."

When she took a breath, the damn sweater fell open. He did not look there. Her serious expression held him, and also made him uncomfortable. All of a sudden, he felt like the bad guy, when he'd never, as far as he knew, hurt anyone on purpose.

"I kissed you because I wanted to," she said. "I find you extremely attractive and hard to resist on a physical level."

"Only physical?"

She waved his question away and let her gaze roam the room.

"My mother basically died of depression, as a direct result of a disappointment too terrible for her mind to accept."

Her gaze lingered on the door. "She had stopped eating, and wouldn't get out of bed. She didn't die here, at home. My mother isn't the ghost I came here to confront. Her ideas are what I need to address, ideas that were pounded into me since the time of the event that kicked her decline into gear."

Chaz swallowed. Should he stop her from digging deep into her secrets, when he had been pushing her for this explanation? Though it wasn't entirely what he had expected, it was also much more than he could have imagined.

"My father left us on Christmas Eve when I was very young," she went on. "He left presents under the tree, as if that would make up for the loss to follow. He walked out without explanation and never looked back, leaving his uneaten dinner on the table. We heard sometime later that he had chosen another family to spend that Christmas morning with, and the rest of his life with after that, which meant that he had cheated on us for some time."

Uncomfortable with her disclosure, Chaz carefully watched Kim readjust her position in the chair and take another long, slow breath.

"I don't do Christmas because my mother hated it, and hated the memory of the night my father left. She never got over the betrayal, and didn't speak to my father again. Neither of us did."

"I see," he said to fill the following pause.

"I've honored my mother's wishes about avoiding this holiday for a long time. So long, I can't remember what life was like before that promise. My mother died six months ago, and since then I've kept up the routine by refusing to celebrate Christmas either in my work or my personal life."

Chaz ran a hand through his hair, feeling like an idiot for pressuring her into admitting a thing like that, and for having almost convinced himself on the way over here that her issues might have derived from something as simple as never getting the gift she asked Santa Claus for. In retrospect, he had failed to give her full credit for having real and serious causes that required the special clause in her contract.

He felt like a heel, and deserved every name she might have called him. The cookies he sent were in a pile of boxes on the floor by his feet. He had brought a tree, planned a party and insisted she go—which made him no better than a goddamn bully.

It was too late for his lame excuses, though as her boss, this was something he had needed to understand. The question now was how much damage he had done to a potential relationship by applying all that pressure?

He kicked a box with his foot and sent it skidding in McKinley's direction. Her gaze moved from the box to him, where her focus stayed.

Chaz was certain the hunger he felt for her was mirrored in her eyes.

* * *

"Will you excuse me a minute?"

Kim got to her feet, fending off two urges at once. The first was to throw herself at Monroe again, no matter the consequences. He stared at her seriously, as if seeing her inner workings for the first time. Kissing him would break the tension in the room and release some of her pent-up emotions after a confession like that.

The second urge was to sprint for the kitchen, close the door and lock herself in.

The latter seemed the best option now that he knew her secrets. If he equated her frank announcement with her recent mental state, it might someday undermine their business relationship. He'd keep an eye out for signs of the same tendency for depression exhibited by her mother, or her threats to pack up and leave. But if that were the case, and he held this against her, Chaz Monroe wasn't worth the shirt on his back.

*Laugh maniacally or cry? Run or break down?*

She wavered among all of those options, having disclosed what haunted her. Her life had been laid bare, the darkness had taken wing, but elation didn't come right away. Some ghosts were clingy.

The way Monroe studied her was sensuously sober, and produced another flicker of heat deep inside her. She had all but begged for him to leave her alone, though she desired the exact opposite. She craved closeness and sharing and mind-bending sex. With Chaz Monroe.

She had bought into her mother's beliefs about men long after they had stopped making sense.

"Suffering isn't supposed to be prolonged, especially this time of year," she said. "Christmas is about joy and light, ideas that might have made a difference to my family if my mother had gritted her teeth and moved on."

Did things have to be so complex? Light...company...

happy times...cookies and a tree. A man beside her to love, and who would love her back unconditionally, loyally and forever. These were what she wanted so badly.

Sex with Monroe wasn't going to get her those things, and yet it somehow seemed a fitting end to the evening. He would hold her. He would be here and make her happy, if only temporarily and for tonight. The main result would be that with his ultramasculine presence in this house, her mother's dark spell over her daughter would be lost, once and for all. She felt that spell already beginning to crack.

To hell with work, her job and how she'd feel tomorrow.

"I'm sorry you had to go through that," he said, getting to his feet, moving to stand beside her.

He didn't touch her and didn't need to. His voice and his tone created a vibration that worked its way down her spine and keep on sliding, finding its way beneath the waistband of her sweatpants and along the curve of her hips to end in a place a vibration had no right to be.

Monroe was no longer the enemy, and she didn't want him to go away. Arguments aside, she felt good around him. She felt completely awake and alive, every nerve tingling, each neuron she possessed calling for her to get closer to him.

"I'm not sure what you'll do with all that," she said, feeling unsteady, unnaturally warm and slightly queasy with him beside her.

The touch came. Only a light one. He tilted her head back with a finger so that she had to look into his eyes. "I'd like to move on to another confidence, one of mine, putting yours aside for now, if you don't mind."

Kim tried to turn her head. He brought her back.

"You do like me, in spite of all this, and all that we've been through so far," he said. "I can feel this. Am I right?"

He went on when she didn't answer. "I want to be near

you. As a matter of fact, I can't seem to stay away. I believe we can make this work. You and me. We can try."

"How? It's already going to be bad when rumor of the scene in the bar spreads. I love my job, and it looks like I'll have to leave it."

"No. Trust me, Kim. Ride this out, and you'll see what can happen. Stick out your tongue at those rumors. I'll take the heat. While I'm in that building, I'll spread my own story about everything being my fault, and we'll make the other employees believe nothing bad happened."

"Nothing did happen."

"It's about to now, I think. Don't you?"

His mouth came close. Kim worked desperately to keep from closing her eyes, needing to see him before feeling the truth of his statement.

"There are more things to disclose in the future about the business that might positively impact your position in the agency. We will get to that, I promise. For now, for to-night, let's enjoy what this is."

His arms encircled her possessively, his warmth persuading her to give in to the rush of need coursing through her body.

She had spoken the magic words to free herself from her mother's tyranny, and she had let a man in. The difference here, between this situation and what happened to her mother, was that she didn't expect any future with Chaz Monroe. If he left that minute, she'd be no worse off because she wasn't fully invested in this liaison producing any kind of relationship and neither was he.

That's what she told herself, anyway, knowing it to be a lie and afraid to admit otherwise. Each minute in Monroe's presence was like one of those holiday gifts she had never received. Being with him brought her some long-awaited anticipation and joy.

"Bedroom," he whispered to her, a world of meaning in that one word.

"No. Not there." Her heart continued to pound. Adrenaline rushed through her to whip up the flames.

They were going to do this.

"Then it will have to be here," he said, swinging her into his arms, kneeling on the floor and placing her there, beside the pile of boxes and bows.

Kim looked up at him, realizing she'd really done it this time. She would soon see all of Chaz Monroe, test her theory on one-night stands being okay for the truly needy, besides being one hell of a spellbreaker…and trust him to take her mind off the rest of the world.

*Just for tonight.*

No one could stop what was about to take place. She craved heat and closeness and for the pain of her family's story to end here, now, completely.

"There's only one problem," she said, pulling him closer.

"What's that?" The mouth hovering over hers held promise in the way it curved up at the corners.

"We have too many clothes in the way," Kim replied with her hands on his chest.

# Fourteen

The kiss was new and intense. Open mouths, damp, darting tongues, breathlessness. There was nothing patient about their need. This wasn't going to be a night of foreplay and tender exploration. They were too excited.

Kim savored the burn of Monroe's closeness, drank him in with each kiss, bite and scratch of her fingernails across the fabric of his shirt. The lid was off the pressure cooker, and she was savage, desirous, anxious for everything he had to give, anxious to find out if it would be enough to permanently keep the ghosts of Christmas past at bay.

In between deep kisses, he gave her time to breathe and searched her face. Their bodies were pressed tightly together, his stretched out on top of hers. His hands were in her hair, on her cheeks, feathering over her neck. Trails of kisses followed each touch of his fingers.

Kim thought she might go mad with her need for him. Her body molded to his, their hips meeting in all the right places as if their bodies were a perfect match. His lips inflicted a torture of the highest caliber, offering promises of what was to come.

When he pulled back, it was only to head south with his incendiary mouth—over her collarbones and over the blue silk covering her breasts. He kissed her there, and she moaned.

She tore at his buttons with impatience. The next sound was of fabric tearing. He had ripped apart the thin ribbon straps of her camisole, exposing her shoulders. Hungrily, he pulled her forward, kissed her again then eased the sweater off and away.

He paused to look at her, his gaze incredibly intimate.

Upright, and without the straps, the silk slid downward over her breasts in a sensuous rustle.

He pressed the palm of one hand against her right breast then cupped her. Kim shut her eyes and began to rock, first backward, then forward. He quickly replaced his hands with his mouth and drew on the pink exposed tip of her breast so deftly, she fought back a cry.

It was too much, and too little. She had never felt anything remotely like this, or wanted so much.

Finding the strength to withstand the pleasure Monroe's mouth gave her, she shoved him back, and with her hands on his buttons, looked at him pleadingly. *No more time. No distractions.*

He understood.

His shirt came off with a twitch and a shrug, baring a muscular chest with a slight dusting of brown hair. As if his magnificent nakedness were a magnet, Kim couldn't keep herself from touching him, running her fingers over him, getting to know every inch from his shoulders to his stomach. He was taut, in perfect shape, the epitome of masculine perfection. But then, she had guessed that from the start.

Aware of her silent approval, Monroe eased her back to the floor and removed her sweatpants in a graceful move that left her shuddering in anticipation. He didn't have time to get to his own pants. She had his belt off and was at his zipper with shaky fingers.

That sexy sound of a zipper opening filled the room. Kim saw only Monroe's face—his expression of lust, his own version of need. Mixed in with those things lay something else: something that she didn't dare put a name to, but knew was reflected in her own expression, and somewhere deep in her body. Deep in her soul.

Chaz Monroe hadn't been kidding. He liked her. He wanted her. His expression said he cared, and that he needed her, at least tonight, as much as she needed him. Knowing this changed things for her, and upped the ante.

He scooped her hips up in both hands and settled himself against her, still looking at her with his eyes wide open. She felt how his muscles tensed. He dipped into her gently at first, easing inside, eyeing her all the while for her reaction.

She had to close her eyes again. Had to. The pleasure of having him inside her was extreme. Suddenly, she wasn't sure if she could handle this, handle him. Already, she felt the rise of a distant rumbling deep inside her body.

He must have felt that rumbling. He used more force after that, entering her with a slick plunge that rocked her to her core. The cry she had withheld escaped.

"I know," he whispered in her ear. "I know."

With strong thighs, he urged her legs to open wider. This time when he entered her moist depths, it was with real purpose. The plunge went deep, forcing another cry to emerge from her swollen mouth.

The internal rumbling gained momentum quickly, hurtling toward where he lay buried inside her, threatening to end what she refused to have finished.

"Can't…" she gasped.

"Yes," he told her. "You can."

His hips began to move, building a rhythm that drove him into her again and again. Her hips matched his, thrust for thrust. Her hands grasped at his bare back, tearing at his flexing muscles with no intent to control his talented ministrations, but to encourage him to proceed, lock him to her, ensure that he wouldn't get away until this was finalized. Until it was over.

The claiming was mutual, necessary and too hot for either of them to prolong. Finally, as time became suspended and the world seemed about to crash down, he drove himself into her one last time…and their startled cries mingled loudly, shockingly, in the room's musty air.

They lay on the floor, quiet and trembling while they caught their breath. Moments later, they started the whole process over again.

# Fifteen

Chaz spiraled in and out of dreams. He wasn't cold, exactly, yet he felt a distant discomfort that forced his eyes open.

He was on his back, on a hard surface. His shoulders ached. So did his knees. Something soft covered him. A blanket?

It took a minute to remember where he was. The room was dark, which meant that not much time had passed since he and Kim had gone at each other.

She wasn't beside him. He sat up, noticing right away that he was buck naked. Their clothes had been discarded completely after round two, in preparation for round three. The edge of a shaggy rug scratched at his thighs.

Kim was gone, but had covered him with a blanket, which was a nice touch. Maybe she preferred a soft mattress to cushion her spent body after a couple hours of sexual gymnastics, and had trotted off to find one. He couldn't really blame her. Then again, she hadn't offered to take him to bed with her, and this threatened to bring on a bout of concern.

Using the coffee table for leverage, Chaz got to his feet. He felt for a lamp on a table next to the sofa and clicked it on. Their clothes were there, strewn across the floor and the chair. Seeing those clothes, Chaz felt slightly better. Kim hadn't tidied up, gotten dressed or removed the outward evidence of their union.

He blew out a breath, unable to recall having spent a night like this in...well, ever. And, he reminded himself, this didn't have to mean love was involved. Great sex amounted to great sex, that's all. Problem was, he wanted her again right that minute. Stranger yet, he desired to hold her, nestle against her, sleep beside her, with Kim curled up in his arms.

This realization came as a shock. Usually the one to grab his clothes and hit the road to terminate a one-night stand, he had stayed, drifting off into a blissful slumber.

And Kim had left him on the floor.

Her absence didn't have to mean she had left him altogether, though. After all, this was her house. So, what did this incredible impulse to nuzzle her imply?

*More trouble ahead.*

The intensity of the sex they'd shared was rare, sure, but did the rest of his urges have to have anything to do with *love?*

*Surely not.* He was merely feeling satisfied and empathetic.

He looked around. The floor was a mess. Piles of cookies had been scattered. Crumbs were everywhere. They had left the tree on the porch. Nothing in this room reflected comfort, really. Kim needed to get out of here. She no longer belonged in this place, and how she felt mattered to him.

She mattered.

His gut tightened. "Kim?" he called out, daring to wake her, needing to disturb her to confirm the new sensations rippling through him.

Finding the stairs, he took them two at a time. Although the hallway at the top lay in darkness, light from below made it possible to see four closed doors and one open doorway. Chaz made for the latter with his heart in his throat.

The blinds in the room were partway open, and the curtains drawn back. By the light from a streetlight, he made out the outline of a bed, a dresser and a light switch, which he flipped on.

Though the bed looked rumpled, Kim wasn't in it.

"Kim?"

No reply came.

He found the bathroom in the hall filled with Kim's scent, but she wasn't there. Back in the hallway, he stopped to listen. The house lay in complete silence.

Bedroom number two was empty, as were the rest of the rooms on that floor. Kim McKinley simply wasn't there.

He'd been jilted. Left. Abandoned in somebody else's house.

And that left him with a very bad feeling about what this meant.

Kim waited by the curb after calling for a cab. Nearly out of breath from hustling to get her act together, she was sloppily dressed in a pair of old jeans, a turtleneck sweater and boots she had found in the closet.

Sore, tired and anxious, she limped back and forth along the sidewalk. The man of her dreams lay on the floor of her mother's living room, surrounded by the cookies he'd brought her. There should have been a law against leaving a man like that, but her first waking instinct had been to flee.

They had broken the house's spell, smashed it to smithereens. And she wanted to run right back inside and do it again, have Monroe again, feel his breath on her face and his naked body against hers.

Breaking old rules had never been so glorious, and at the same time confusing. She hadn't made love to him in order to plan for a future of bedrooms and kitchens. She looked for companionship and warmth on a chilly night, a temporary relationship worthy of blasting away the past. Well, she had found those things. Too much of those things.

She was doing the walking-away routine. As hard as that was and as bad as she felt about it, she had to leave. Monroe might be one hell of a guy, but leaving him now meant he wouldn't have the chance to leave her later or be afforded the opportunity to break her heart. Monroe would cause trouble in her future if she stuck around, because she really, really liked him. She wanted him badly. More than ever. She needed iron willpower in order to remain on the street.

What would he do when he woke up in a strange house, alone? Curse? Get angry?

She wasn't going to see that reaction now or in the future. In the aftermath of shared confidences, confessions and a night of raw animal sex, being in the same business, in the same building, would be out of the question. No way would she be able to hide her hunger for Chaz Monroe after tonight. If she caved on this point, she'd be setting herself up for a fall.

She felt as though she'd had a taste of the fall already. Her chest hurt. The inner fires still raged.

When the cab pulled up, Kim took one more glance at the dark house before giving the driver her destination and some special instructions. Then she climbed into the backseat. With Monroe off-limits from now on, she'd at least have a keepsake. A trophy to remember this night by...as if she could ever forget it.

*It's okay. I'll be all right.*

The hurt of leaving Monroe would stop eventually. With her mother's hold broken, she was free to sell this house and enjoy the things she had shunned. Acknowledgment of that gave her a sense of freedom.

Having made the decision to part company with Monroe and get on with her life, she'd be embracing the phrase *starting over.* Monroe had helped with that. "Thank you," Kim whispered as the cab headed for the city.

Halfway there, her tears began to pool.

Damn if she didn't miss him already.

Chaz didn't want to focus on the phrase that came to mind as he sat down on a step in Kim's mother's house.

*The little vixen used me?*

After years of dating, he'd been jilted after the best night of his life. By the only woman he wanted in his life.

*How did that happen?*

Could he have been wrong about her? Wrong about how fully she'd enjoyed the sex and his company? No one had that kind of ability to fake the pleasure of round after round of mind-blowing physical connection. No, Kim had thoroughly enjoyed what they'd done. She'd participated, wanting that union as much as he had. Tears had stained her cheeks once or twice, and that had damn near broken his heart.

What about the blanket she'd covered him with? Was that the action of someone who had faked her way through an entire evening, possibly with an ulterior motive or secret agenda?

*Can't see that.*

So, if she had gotten as much pleasure out of their evening together as he did, why had she gone, and where?

Chaz glanced at his watch. *Two o'clock in the morning.*

In a few hours, he had a meeting with some bankers to discuss the possibilities of a future sale, a meeting that had been set up before he stepped foot inside the agency, and before he'd first caught sight of Kim's enviable backside in the corridor. Her disappearance sidelined the opportunity to tell her about his plans for the future sale of the company. Likely she had left him believing it imperative for one of them to go. The way she left, without a word, presented only one scenario. Kim was saying goodbye to all of it—the job and him.

"Well, that sucks," he muttered, looking around the room where they had *merged.* An appropriate term for what they had done, as many times as they'd done it, since they hadn't taken the time or the precision necessary for it to have been called *making love.*

*Making love* would have meant something more than casual sex. The thing that came after all the lust had been explored, involving slow exploration and much softer kisses.

Tonight had been about casual sex between consenting adults. Right?

All of a sudden, he wasn't so sure.

His spirit took a dive.

He wanted her back.

Kim McKinley had one-upped him again in a game he had no longer planned to play. Regretting that, Chaz looked to the front door, then to his clothes on the floor.

So, okay, he had tried and lost. He had lost *her*. He'd live. Monroes were champion survivors. Buying and selling businesses hardened his anti-relationship stamina, and he had every intention of learning to deal with the consequences.

In need of air, he picked up his pants and dressed. Opening the front door, hoping Kim might be on the porch, his stomach took a tumble when she wasn't.

But he paused in the doorway, heat shooting up the back of his neck. He grinned. Something about that porch seemed different, and that difference told him this wasn't over.

The silky-skinned little siren might have fled, yes. But she'd taken the Christmas tree with her.

Kim woke exhausted and achingly sore in every muscle after two full days of recuperation time from her evening with Monroe. The sense of being perpetually on the edge of a state of anxiousness refused to leave her. Her heart continued to race. Her ears rang.

Not her ears. The cell phone on her table by the bed made the racket.

After rolling onto her side, she checked the caller ID, holding the phone aloft while it continued to screech. The screen said the call came from a private number. Letting it go to voice mail, she tossed the phone to the foot of the bed and stretched out on her back. She had nowhere special to be on day three of her plan to not only eradicate the sadness of the past, but to obliterate it, too.

Her fingers slid sideways to the empty spot next to her on the mattress, then recoiled. *He* wasn't there. No one was. Funny how real dreams could be.

Her project for today was to make another attempt at forgetting Chaz Monroe, which had so far proved difficult. She'd spent another mostly sleepless night thinking about what to do next and trying to erase all thoughts of him. Each time she closed her eyes, he was there, strong, handsome and tenacious. Last night, six cups of strong black tea had been necessary to keep her eyes open and the memory of him controlled.

Her body now paid for the lack of sleep, as well as the antics of her hours spent with Monroe on a hardwood floor, by offering up protests, bruises and stiffness whenever she moved. Monroe had deliciously involved every part of her body, over and over, until she thought she might perish in a state of pure, blissful pleasure. Being manhandled by him had been outrageously satisfying.

But that was in the past.

Today was all about new beginnings that didn't include Monroe or his advertising agency. This was about her, moving on.

And what was the best way to take a break from reality? *Shop.*

She planned to pile on new sensations, spend some of her savings and revel in the freedom of a new mind-set.

Today was the first day of the rest of her...

She sat straight up.

Somebody knocked at the door.

Scrambling out of bed, wincing with each movement of her tender thighs, Kim limped to the door. The visitor had to be a neighbor, or Sam would have let her know. Maybe it was Brenda, who had her own key, and therefore didn't really have to knock, except out of politeness and to prevent Kim from having a heart attack.

Through the peephole she saw Brenda, chic and festive in a dark green suit.

Kim opened the door. "I don't actually want a gossip hour today, Bren, unless you've heard of a decent job opportunity through the grapevine *and* brought breakfast along. I'm starved."

Brenda gave her a pained look, pursed her mouth and stepped aside.

Traitorous Brenda wasn't alone.

Surprised, Kim stepped back with her heart hammering.

"I have a line of gossip I think will interest you," Monroe said in the husky voice that always made her knees weak and made them weak now.

Kim blinked, and looked to Brenda.

"It's news you truly might like," Brenda seconded. "You can kick me later for delivering it this way."

Though she tried hard not to look at Monroe, the strength of his presence drew her like a suicidal moth to an impenetrable flame.

# Sixteen

Monroe stood on her doorstep, looking like every woman's idea of a prebreakfast treat.

Dressed to impress in soft gray pants, black leather jacket and another blue shirt that matched his eyes to perfection, he stared back, his expression a mixture of stoicism and worry.

After denying herself the luxury of purposefully giving in to her thoughts about him for the last couple days, Kim's first instinct was to jump his bones. From a distance of three feet, he smelled like heaven.

Her inner alarm system went to full alert. She said firmly, "You understand the meaning of the term *vacation?*"

"I'll explain if given the chance," he said.

"Do I actually have to be here?" Brenda interjected. "I have a meeting in twenty minutes. You two can work this out without me."

"You brought him here," Kim reminded her friend. "This one's on you."

"Wrong," Brenda argued with a shake of her head. "It's quite possibly all about *you,* and I'm merely the middleman *again.*"

"I'm in my pajamas, Bren."

"I didn't notice," Monroe said lightly, lying through his teeth. His eyes continued to roam over every inch of her anatomy, from her head to her bare feet.

She crossed her arms to cover herself, hoping to delay the quick-rising crave factor from reaching her breasts.

"I've been calling you for the past fifteen minutes, to warn you that we were on our way," Brenda said.

Kim glanced over her shoulder as if she could see her cell phone through the wall. "From another cell?"

Brenda nodded. "Mine's at the office. We left in a hurry."

"How was I supposed to know you were calling?"

Brenda threw up her hands. "I don't know. Psychically?"

Brenda was usually connected to her phone at the hip, so for her not to have it meant that Monroe had dragged her here. As what, a buffer or a mediator?

Kim confronted Monroe with narrowed eyes. "You can't come in."

"I'm having a déjà-vu moment in this hallway," he remarked, "when I thought we were beyond that."

His meaning wasn't lost on her. Yes, they were beyond it, if their recent nakedness and exchange of body fluids meant he had a free pass to bother her anytime he wanted to.

Kim felt the flush spread up her neck and into her cheeks. Her sore thighs were heating up, as if she were more than willing to go another round on any surface with the man across from her.

Managing to tear her gaze from him, Kim looked to her friend. "Go on. You wanted to tell me something important enough to bring him along?"

Brenda nodded. "His plans were to sell the agency after getting it up and running and more profitable. That's what his family does. They buy and sell businesses, and they've made a fortune doing so."

Brenda tossed a glance Monroe's way before continuing. He remained mute.

"If he sells the agency, you'll still have the opportunity to be promoted, and he will be gone, so no worries there about pesky rumors or anything else. It looks like all this is in your favor," Brenda said. "I trespassed on your vacation time to tell you this so you won't plan on leaving the agency, or town. You don't have to. Not now. Plus, I wasn't supposed to tell anyone, so the boss decided to come along when I did."

Kim's gaze bounced back to Monroe. "Is this true?"

He nodded. "Yes, it is."

"You never planned on owning the agency for long, or being there long-term?"

"That was the initial plan," he replied. "I was going to tell you about this the other night, but we got distracted."

*Distracted? Seriously? That's what he called it?*

"This is the news you said you'd postpone until later?" Kim asked.

"Yes," he said.

"You didn't think it was important enough to bring up right away?"

"There were other issues to deal with first."

Admittedly, the news should have made her feel better. She should have jumped for joy. She didn't have to leave the job she loved. She just had to make it work, or prolong the vacation until Monroe sold the place. Instead of feeling relief, though, her stomach churned.

Chaz Monroe would be gone.

The last few days of her life passed before her eyes. Monroe hadn't really taken the VP spot but had simply gone undercover in his own business to help it along on the road to full financial recovery. She didn't have to worry about him in the future, as far as work went, because he wasn't going to be there to give her hot flashes each time they passed in the corridors.

And the part of this situation that had bitten her in the backside—the contractual issue—was ebbing away due to having confronted her mother's ghosts.

She was nothing like her mother. Not even a bit. She had a lot to look forward to.

Monroe's news was good, all right, though it also left them both on uneven ground. If he left the agency and wanted to see her, there'd be no more excuses to stay away from him. In truly shedding her mother's fears, there'd be no need to stay away from him. If he left the agency, she might *want* to see him, often, and would be free to do so, if that one small fear didn't remain about being left behind after giving her love to a man.

"Kim?" Brenda said.

Does that meet with your approval?" he asked. "I'll soon be out of your hair, and you can pursue the promotion any way you'd like to."

Out of her hair?

Her stomach constricted. The words were like a blow.

His comment didn't sound as though it came from a man ready to pursue a relationship with her.

She'd been fantasizing about him for nothing?

Kim closed her eyes. *Fool.*

Maybe he'd already gotten what he wanted from her, with no plans for furthering their connection. A male victory. A conquest.

His expression had become guarded. He hadn't made the slightest move in her direction, or agreed with Brenda's suggestion that she leave them alone to work this out.

Because there was nothing to work out?

Kim staggered back a few inches, struck by the pathetic degree of her own vulnerability. *I haven't learned anything.*

"Fine," she said softly. "Good."

Then she closed the door in Monroe's face.

She leaned against the frame, gathering her wits, bolstering her courage to be the new Kim McKinley she had only three days ago set out to be, while sensing Monroe's presence through the closed door.

"I take it she wasn't happy with the news," he said in the hallway.

"She was in her pajamas," Brenda remarked, as if that fact explained everything.

"Well, I'm done here. I've given up trying to determine what might make her happy," Monroe said. "I went out of my way to reconcile, with every intention of helping her out, but I'm no idiot. She's on her own. Come on. I'll walk back to the office with you. Sorry you came along without a coat. It's cold outside, so you can use mine."

"Hell, Monroe," Brenda said. "You can be downright chivalrous when you want to. If you weren't in love with my best friend, I might want to date you."

"Love?" Monroe said. "I think you must be a true romantic, Brenda."

"Your eyes lingered."

"I'm a man, and she was in her pajamas."

"You can't fool anybody, Monroe, except maybe yourself."

Their voices faded, but the comments rang in Kim's ears like an echo. *Love?* How little Brenda knew about what had happened, and about Monroe's subsequent victory.

He had given up, thrown in the towel. Why did his proclamation send icy chills through her overheated system?

The other night, everything she dared to want had been within her grasp, yet she hadn't reached for it, needing to be strong on her own terms. Now some of those happy endings were no longer viable, and only the stuff of dreams.

She was sick to death of what-ifs and games and hypothetical problem solving. Monroe had given up without a word to her about their night together and how he felt about it, personally. He'd needed to accompany Brenda here; there was a chance he wouldn't have come on his own.

He hadn't agreed with Brenda about loving her, or mentioned anything other than wanting to help her to get the promotion she deserved.

*A professional visit, then.*
*Not personal at all.*
*Nothing remotely resembling love.*

All right. She'd have to make that work, and for now occupy her time elsewhere. Keep busy, and on the right path. Back to shopping. She'd indulge every other whim to its maximum potential. This would make her feel better and blur the emptiness deep inside that Chaz Monroe had temporarily filled.

Pondering how many times in the last seventy-two hours she'd arrived at the same conclusion, Kim headed for her closet to dump the pajamas. There was some serious *forget-him* therapy to do, and no time to waste.

"Who am I kidding?" she whispered, dropping to her bed with her head in her hands. "What we had felt like love to me."

It was insane. Possibly the worst idea she'd ever come up with. Nevertheless, it was what a mature grown-up would do.

Her dress was black, short, sleeveless, with a moderately cut neckline and a perfectly fitted waist. She covered it with a fur-trimmed sweater and added a string of crystal beads at her throat. Her shoes were black Louboutin knockoffs with tall, gold heels that significantly increased her height and lent her an air of confidence that came with overspending.

She sat in the cab, eyeing the big house with determination, and took a few deep breaths before emerging on a cobbled driveway bordered by a knee-high hedge. The mansion was aglow with bright golden light. Windows and doors glittered handsomely, welcomingly. Garlands of evergreen and holly swooped in perfect loops, tied with red velvet bows and dripping with colored glass balls. Rows of cars lined the driveway, as well as part of the street.

What would growing up in a house like this have been like? She hadn't thought to ask Monroe where he lived now, and it no longer mattered, anyway. Ten days had passed since he last stood in her hallway, declaring his decision to give up on helping her further. Ten miserable days. She hadn't been back to the office yet, since her projects had been completed before she'd taken a break. Time and distance away from Monroe had been necessary in order to contemplate her future.

So, here she was, at Monroe's parents' home, about to attend a Christmas party she was supposed to have helped design. It was Christmas Eve, and she was here as she'd promised Monroe she would be, before the rift with him widened. Coming here was a big step, but doable, now that she was getting used to the idea of going it alone.

She would smile at Monroe, and maybe shake hands. They'd share a laugh over how silly they both had been. She'd wish him well with the sale of the agency.

The front door of the house stood wide open, manned by a greeter in a black suit holding a silver tray of sparkling champagne flutes. Kim took a glass as she entered the expansive foyer with its warmly aged wood floors, mirrors and framed oil paintings of lush landscapes.

People of all ages were everywhere. Children raced through the foyer, and back and forth into adjoining rooms, laughing, teasing, having a good time. She envied them. Christmas was magical for children, and this party exemplified that magic to perfection.

If the exterior radiated glow and welcome, the interior of the Monroe house magnified that. Kim knew what the living room would look like before entering, and found it exactly like the rendering she'd seen. Ice sculptures towered over plates of food on center tables. Foam snow whitened windowsills. There was gilt tableware and crystal. Best of all, the largest tree she'd ever seen took up one full corner, at least ten feet of greenery loaded with decorations, twinkling lights and dangling candy canes.

Though she expected this kind of sensory wonderland, the sight stopped her. Her eyes filled, and she choked back a sob. The room was unbearably beautiful. For a holiday-starved woman only now overcoming the past, the magic seemed overwhelming.

Her hands began to tremble. Champagne sloshed from her glass. Would Monroe find her? Welcome her? Save her from all this beauty by snapping her back to reality?

A subtle movement, singled out from the comings and goings of the people around her, caught her eye. A man stood in the opposite doorway, leaning casually against the jamb. He was dressed in a tasteful black sweater and pants and wore a look of casual unconcern. Kim's heart skidded inside her rib cage. She almost spilled more of her drink.

But it wasn't Monroe who raised his glass at her. It wasn't Monroe who smiled, or Monroe's eyes that took her in. Similar in height and weight, and nearly as handsome, with the same dark hair and fair face, whoever this was pushed off the wall and headed in her direction when their gazes connected.

The lights suddenly seemed too bright, too real, too magical. In the middle of the wonderful holiday glitter she'd only began to wrap her mind around, dealing with another man who looked like Monroe, but wasn't, became too much for Kim to handle.

She should not have come. She wasn't ready.

Setting her glass on the table, she turned. Before the man could reach her, she'd reached the foyer, and with just one more look over her shoulder at the luxurious wonderland that was Monroe's life, she exited quickly, and as silently as she had arrived.

"Rory?" Chaz said, finding his brother in the foyer looking perplexed.

"You missed it, bro," Rory said, staring at the door.

"What did I miss?"

"Only the most gorgeous creature on the planet."

Chaz grinned. "There are a lot of beautiful women here tonight."

"Not like this one."

"By the way, how much champagne have you chugged? Have we run out yet?"

"I'm serious," Rory said. "She was a vision."

Chaz looked past his brother. "So, where is this goddess?"

"She left."

"The party just started," Chaz pointed out.

"That's what makes her exit so dramatic."

"Sorry you lost her so soon, bro."

"I didn't imagine her, Chaz."

"Sorry," Chaz repeated, ready to get another drink in order to catch up with Rory, and intending to drown his sorrows.

Rory's laugh was self-deprecating. "Well, I suppose there is another blonde here somewhere with an alluring hazel-eyed gaze and a body like sin. If so, I plan to find her."

Chaz experienced a slight bump in his drinking plan, but couldn't have explained why. "Hazel eyes?" he echoed.

"Yeah. Aren't we all suckers for eyes like that?"

Chaz had to ask, knowing the question to be ridiculous, but unable to beat off the strange feeling in his gut. "Did she wear a red dress?"

Rory shook his head. "A little black number that fit like a glove. But hey, this isn't all about women. Tonight's for celebrating. You've found potential buyers for the agency, I hear, and they'll wait six months to decide to move forward on a sale if you get the place running smoothly."

"Yes. I suppose that's good news."

"Suppose? Chaz, it's your first big deal. Shall we have a toast?"

That bit of odd intuition returned and clung. Chaz couldn't seem to shake it off.

"Did she have hair about to here?" He touched his shoulder. "And long legs?"

"You did see her, then?" Rory replied teasingly. "I didn't imagine her in some Christmas-related state of hopefulness?"

"Was she alone?" Chaz pressed.

"I wouldn't be pining if she'd had a guy by her side."

Chaz barely heard Rory. He was already out the front door and thinking that if it could have been McKinley…

If there was any way it might have been Kim, and she had made the effort to show up here after all…

Did that mean she was interested? Had she hoped to find him?

He didn't see her on the portico or in the yard.

*Hell…* Wasn't there an old fairy tale about finding a shoe on the steps that would fit only one person on the planet? Which would help to narrow things down a bit for a poor, lovesick guy tired of pretending he didn't give a fig about the woman who owned that shoe, when he cared a whole frigging lot?

When he, Chaz Monroe, cared about Kim McKinley so much, he felt empty without her?

His keys were in his pocket. His car was parked in front of the garage. Waving people out of the way, uttering quick words of greeting and something vague about an emergency, he got in, started the engine and stepped on the gas.

# Seventeen

Chaz couldn't get past Sam, no matter how hard he tried.

"No, sir. Not tonight. Strict orders to let no one in, on the threat of ending my life as I know it."

Kim wouldn't answer her phone. At first Chaz thought that she might not have come home, but at last, Sam, sensing a desperate man's weakness and caught up in the holiday spirit, confirmed she was indeed up there.

"Hate to see her alone on a fine night like this," Sam said.

All Chaz thought about was seeing her. She had come to the party, showed up on his parents' doorstep, and he'd somehow missed her. Rotten luck. But she hadn't stayed long enough for him to find her. According to Rory, she'd dashed out the door. So here he was, with his heart thundering way above the norm, determined to see Kim tonight. And as he paced in front of her building, looking up, there seemed only one way to accomplish that…if he didn't get arrested first.

The fire escape.

Floor six. Several windows down ought to be hers, but it was possible he'd gotten turned around. That window virtually beamed with flashes of red and green light emulating the wattage of an alien spaceship trapped in a tunnel.

Could that be her window?

The only thing left now was to scoot over, ledge by ledge, until he reached that one. Briefly, he wondered if Santa had a fear of heights.

He slipped twice, caught himself and began to sweat, despite the chill factor. Glancing down, he swore beneath his breath and continued, placing one foot on the ledge outside where he thought he needed to go.

The light in that window was blinding, so it couldn't be hers. If it was, she'd had a major turnaround, and he was going to need sunglasses.

He got his second foot on the ledge and reached the window unscathed. Maintaining a fairly tight hold on the brick, he craned his neck and peeked around the corner.

The light came from a tree, lit up and glowing. There had to be twenty strings of lights on that tree. Tinsel dangled like silver icicles. Gold and silver baubles gleamed.

But that wasn't all.

Candles lit other surfaces, one of them on the sill not twelve inches away from where he clung. The wonderful scent of cinnamon wafted to him through the closed window.

*This can't be hers.*

*All this?*

Yet somehow he knew it was, and that if she had progressed to this degree on the serious issues, where did that leave him?

The truth hit him like a blow to the gut as he looked inside that window. He loved Kim McKinley for this.

He loved her for showing up at the party, and for that room full of lights. He loved her beautiful face, the graceful slope of her shoulders, her bare feet, berry-colored toenails, and her slightly haughty attitude when she got angry. He loved the big eyes that held the power to make a grown man, a confirmed bachelor, climb a fire escape in the middle of winter.

Come to think of it, he didn't need a tally of all the things he loved about her. There were just too many things to list.

His heart ached to be inside of that apartment with her, and to know everything else about her, down to the smallest detail—all the stuff, bad and good, sickness and health.

He put a hand to his head to make sure it was still screwed on tight, sure he'd never felt like this, or considered the *M* word before. Yet he was seeing a future with Kim McKinley that included a ring.

He grinned. Rory was going to have a heart attack.

The only thing now was to convince Kim to take him back, and to remain by his side. *Forever* seemed like a good place to start.

Though elated over this decision, Chaz did not raise a victory fist to the moon, which would have been a dangerous move for a man stuck to a ledge six floors above pavement, wearing entirely unacceptable clothes for the weather. And it was time to go before someone called the cops. He'd bribe Sam to plead on his behalf for Kim to let him in. He would take Sam with him to her front door if necessary. Just one more look in this window, then, he swore to God, he'd go.

He pressed his face close to the pane...

And nearly fell backward when Kim peered back.

Kim stepped away, stifling the urge to scream. There was a man outside her window, and she had to call the cops.

But the face looking in was familiar.

"Monroe?" she said in disbelief.

He grinned. "Just trying this fire escape out to see if it will hold Santa, and wondering why cops never go after him."

The sight of Monroe on the other side of her window made her blink slowly. "What do you want?"

"You left the party without saying hello."

"I made a mistake thinking I could handle the party."

"The mistake was to flee before I could stop you."

Kim shook her head. "Why are you out there?"

"Why did you give Sam orders to shoot me on sight?"

"I wanted to suffer alone."

He took a beat to reply to that. "Suffer?"

"Go away, Chaz."

"I have a better idea. Why don't you let me in?"

"For one thing, I haven't been able to open this window since I moved in."

He stared at her thoughtfully. "How about if I knock on your door?"

"You haven't answered my first question about what you want," Kim said. Her heart was leaping frantically. Monroe was on the fire escape. He had left the party and come here to see her. This had to mean he wanted to see her pretty badly.

When he didn't answer, she repeated the question. "What do you want, Chaz?"

He shrugged without losing his balance and said, "You. I want you. And you just called me Chaz."

And then he was gone, and Kim didn't think she could move from the spot. He hadn't given up. If this was some particularly nasty joke, and the business needed her for something...

*Would he do that?*

She couldn't have read his expression incorrectly—that look of longing in his eyes that probably looked exactly like her own.

She'd been halfway out of her dress, and yanked it back over her shoulders. She pressed the hair back from her face and looked at the tree and the trimmings that had set her bank account back more than the dress and shoes combined.

What would Chaz do now that he had seen how she embraced Christmas? That the tree he brought her had made her happy, despite the thought of losing him.

The call came. Her hand shook when she told Sam to let Chaz come up. She waited by the door, planning what to say first. Maybe she'd start by asking him to repeat what he said about wanting her, just to be sure he meant it.

She opened the door before he knocked, unable to wait or keep calm. Chaz stood there with his hand raised. He reached for her instead.

He held her tightly for several seconds before pushing her back through the door. The momentum carried them to her kitchen, where he paused long enough to look at her and smile.

"This isn't what you think it is," he said.

"Damn." Heat flooded Kim's face as she smiled back.

"You want it to be what you think it is?" he asked.

"Yes," she answered breathlessly.

He closed his eyes briefly. Then he kissed her, long, deep and thoroughly, with his body tight to hers. After that, he kissed her again and again, as if he had saved up longing and had to get it out.

When he drew back to allow her a breath, he said, "You have a tree."

"Yes."

"You came to the party."

"I did."

"You were looking for me?"

"Yes."

"Because you wanted to be with me? Had to be with me? Could no longer picture a life without me in it?"

"Yes. Yes. And yes."

When Chaz smiled again, his eyes lit up with emotion. She saw relief, joy and the finality of having found something he was sure he'd lost. Genuine feelings. Very personal stuff.

"What do you think of the word *love?*" he asked quietly.

"Highly overrated," she said with a voice that quavered.

"Unless it covers us?" he suggested.

"Does it cover us?"

"I believe so."

"When will you know for sure?"

"As soon as you take me to that bedroom. The one all lit up like the North Pole."

"That's sex, not love."

"To my way of thinking, the two are mutually beneficial. Am I wrong?"

She shook her head. "Isn't there some kind of law against naked bodies under a Christmas tree?"

"Oh, I don't think so. Definitely not. So let's make love, Kim, beside that tree and under the lights. Let's slow down and create a path to the future that will suit us both."

It was the defining moment, and Kim knew it. The future Chaz spoke of had to be built on trust and understanding. She must believe he would make good on those things. In return, she'd have to do the same. She'd have to believe him, and believe in a future with him.

He pressed a kiss on her forehead and another on her cheek. His hands wrapped around her, warm through her dress, as he pulled her to him possessively.

Her world spun off into blissful chaos. Goose bumps trickled down her spine. A rush of delight closed her eyes tight.

Each glorious inch his lips traveled over hers left a trail of fire, the same raging flames she'd felt before, though this time, he also ran a hand down her bare arm, to her wrist. He clasped her fingers in his and held her hand.

Something so simple. So defining and rich. Better than anything. Two promises in one. She wasn't alone. Together, they would get through this, and be better for it.

Kim's shoulders twitched. Her hips ground to his hips as she kissed him back, matching his hunger with hers and forgetting everything else but the desire to have this man inside her, and with her always.

She was going to take this chance. She was going to trust Chaz Monroe because she loved him.

She moaned into his waiting mouth. With a tight hold on her hand, he turned and led her toward the lights.

"The best Christmas ever," he said over his shoulder.

# Eighteen

"Kim?" Brenda called out from her cubicle, standing up quickly. "What happened? I haven't seen you for days. I haven't heard from you."

"I didn't get fired," Kim said with a straight face.

"He left a message on your desk about wanting to see you the minute you came in."

"Yes. I have to sign a new contract."

"He convinced you?"

"He's one hell of a negotiator, Bren."

"You'll fill me in, won't you? There's something strange in your expression. Not at all like a woman having lost a battle of wills. It's going to be okay, isn't it? You're going to stay?"

Kim nodded. "I'm staying."

"I knew you could work it out," Brenda said, showing major relief.

Kim took the longest strides her tight skirt allowed, stopping in her cubicle just long enough to open a drawer and retrieve something she had stored there, before heading down the corridor to Chaz's office.

Alice didn't stop her or offer up a protest. Instead, Alice smiled, and nodded her head.

Kim didn't bother to make a pretense of knocking or waiting to be asked to come in. This was her déjà-vu moment, and she intended to experience it to the fullest. Things had changed. She had changed, and felt downright hopeful about the future.

Her heart beat thunderously, tellingly, as she opened the door. The anticipation of seeing Chaz was always like that, and had grown worse over the last few days of spending nearly every waking minute with him. She'd been wearing a smile since his daring use of her fire escape.

He wasn't at his desk. She waited, pulse soaring, body anticipating the onslaught of sensation.

She didn't have to wait long.

All of a sudden he grabbed her by the wrist and swung her around. The door closed. The lock clicked.

His warm mouth covered hers immediately, and her lips opened in a ravenous response. Warm tongues danced. His hands explored possessively, already knowing what they would find. She had lost count of the number of times they had made love lately, but the vast number was a dizzying indication of shared feelings. They had talked, too, and laughed. Together, they had banished the dark and let in the light.

His incredibly steamy kiss was indicative of his new need for her. She wanted to protest when the treacherous bastard peeled his lips from hers way too soon and began to hum a tune that turned out to be a slightly off-key rendition of "Jingle Bells."

Several seconds passed before Kim said, "See? I'm cured. And that's behind us now." Then she began to laugh. All the emotion of the past had just melted away. They had made Christmas wonderful; a time never to forget.

Chaz laughed with her as he began to raise her skirt. She loved that he never had enough of her. That's the way she liked it. She loved everything about him, too. This was love at its most exhilarating.

But she placed her hands on his hands to stop his progress.

"We won't do this kind of thing in my future office," she said.

"Luckily, it's still mine," he countered. "And I have no such rules."

"We already did it this morning."

"Are you tired of me already?"

"What if they still say I slept my way to the top?"

"I'll agree."

Kim cuffed his shoulder then ran her hand along the seam of his perfectly ironed shirt, looking for a way inside. There was something hard in his shirt pocket. A tiny box.

She glanced up at him.

"I'm pretty sure I can't show this to you yet," he said, his grin firmly in place. "Seems too pushy. Too desperate. And after all, as the owner of this agency, I have a reputation to maintain."

Kim waited this out, anticipating a punch line.

"But I have another present for you today, one that you might not have noticed."

She raised an eyebrow, nervous and excited about the contents of the box in his pocket.

"To see the other surprise, you'll have to open that door again," Chaz said. "The one you just waltzed through."

"I'm kind of content right here," she protested.

"Well, then… Have you ever made love on a desk?" he asked teasingly.

Faking a fluster, Kim smoothed her skirt down and turned to open the door. She saw right away what she had missed on her way in, and her heart again began to thump. In black paint, outlined in gold, was her name, printed on the glass. *Kim McKinley, Vice President.*

It took her a full minute to realize this was going to be true.

"I've decided to hang on to the place for a while," Chaz said. "So I'll need someone I can trust in this office while I pursue other interests."

Kim stared at the name on the door. After that, she looked to Alice, who was smiling. She looked to Chaz, also smiling. Heat began to drift over her. Way down deep in her body, in a place reserved for his touch, a drum beat started up.

Chaz Monroe was going to trust her with this promotion in a company he had decided to keep, at least for now, and hopefully long enough for her to prove herself. Waves of happiness washed over her. She squeezed her eyes shut to contain her joy.

"I won't be around much, so rumors about us won't matter," he said.

Kim didn't open her eyes. This Christmas, her wishes had come true. She had the job, and a relationship with the man beside her. That was all she needed. She could do this. Mutual trust was a beautiful thing.

"Will you say yes?" Chaz asked.

Her eyes again met his.

"About the office," he clarified, his voice dropping to a whisper that told her he meant something else entirely.

She nodded.

He smiled.

"You're an asset to the company, Kim Monroe," he said. "Come on, let's take a good look at your future desk, and see if there might be anything else you'll need to put on it."

It wasn't until he pressed her across that desk with his arms around her that Kim dropped her stranglehold on the golden plaque she'd fished from her drawer. She'd soon be able to use the plaque that announced her new position in the agency.

Vice President.

She didn't have to toss it away or wave it in his face.

Only then did she realize what he'd said. The name he had spoken. *Kim Monroe?*

He placed a finger over her lips to stop her from commenting. His eyes shone a merry, vivid blue. "Good. Great. Terrific," he said. "More on that later, and plenty of time for that conversation. Just now, I find that I can't let you waste another good, overheated breath."

The kiss, probably the hundredth like it since she had met Chaz, each of them better than the first, told her all she needed to know. He was not only going to trust her with the business, he was going to trust that she'd stay with him forever, too.

And the desk she had coveted for so long was as fitting a place as any to seal that new bargain.

"Happy New Year, my love," Chaz said in a scintillating whisper before he proceeded to make good on the meaning of the sentiment.

\* \* \* \* \*